## GAMADGE HAD ARRIVED
## JUST A LITTLE TOO LATE . . .

They stood looking into the dim room. Mrs. Wakes had not put her papers away or covered her type-writer. Gamadge had not moved from the doorway; now he went across the room and bent over the figure on the couch.

"Out like a light," said the superintendent. "Early for her."

Mrs. Wakes looked as though she had barely made the trip to the day bed. She had sat down, leaned back against the pillow, and gone to sleep with her feet on the floor. Gamadge lifted her hand.

Gamadge sat in the wicker chair and looked at Mrs. Wakes. She had had a quiet death.

## THE BOOK OF THE LION

# THE BOOK
# OF
# THE LION

## Elizabeth Daly

**BANTAM BOOKS**
TORONTO • NEW YORK • LONDON • SYDNEY • AUCKLAND

THE BOOK OF THE LION

*A Bantam Book / published by arrangement with
Holt, Rinehart & Winston General Book*

*PRINTING HISTORY*
*First published in Great Britain 1951*
*Bantam edition / May 1985*

ISBN 0-553-24883-9

*Bantam Books are published by Bantam Books, Inc. Its trademark,
consisting of the words "Bantam Books" and the portrayal of a rooster,
is Registered in U.S. Patent and Trademark Office and in other
countries. Marca Registrada. Bantam Books, Inc., 666 Fifth Avenue,
New York, New York 10103.*

# Contents

# 1

# Life and Letters

The telephone rang, and Gamadge leaned forward across his desk blotter—and across his yellow cat Martin— to pick up the receiver. Martin, lying stretched out on his side, asleep, did not open his eyes. He paid no attention to telephone bells. He was old, so old that nobody disturbed him any more.

As Gamadge leaned back again, receiver at his ear, Martin half awoke, and caught at Gamadge's sleeve with a languid claw. As the sleeve receded, the claw disentangled itself and dropped away.

"Take it easy," said Gamadge, and addressed the telephone: "Gamadge speaking."

He was sleepy himself. He had been looking up the sales history of an old book in old catalogues, and there was nothing about the job to keep him wakeful. Nothing in his surroundings, either—the quiet of the office, the low fire in the grate, the timelessness of a rainy day. It was Monday, the fifth of May, 1947; and so far the Spring of 1947 had been moist and chill.

A businesslike feminine voice at the other end of the wire prodded him back to actuality: "This is Mr. Henry Gamadge?"

"Yes."

"One moment, please."

Gamadge sat well down on the end of his spine, legs stretched out, eyes vacant.

Another feminine voice, clear and refined, came on the wire: "Mr. Henry Gamadge?"

"Right here."

"One moment, please."

Gamadge was annoyed. Not having anybody at the moment to do this for him to other people, he didn't like other people to do it to him. He said: "Be here when you want me," stretched across Martin, and replaced the telephone. Martin, eyes half open, lifted his paw, decided against effort, and let the paw fall.

Gamadge remained sitting forward, his eyes on a catalogue, a pencil in his fingers. The telephone rang.

"Mr. Gamadge?"

"Still here."

"We were cut off."

"Too bad."

"I am speaking for Mr. Avery Bradlock, of Ferris, Bradlock and Charles. Investment securities."

This ancient and honourable company had not only weathered all storms in the past, but had almost given the impression of ignoring them. Gamadge said: "Oh, yes."

"Mr. Bradlock would be very glad if you would make an appointment to come down and see him, Mr. Gamadge. Tomorrow, if possible. Unless you *could* make it to-day? The Wall Street office, you know."

Gamadge asked: "What does Mr. Bradlock want to see me about?"

The voice rebuked him coldly: "Mr. Bradlock will tell you that."

"You don't know?"

"Of course I do not know."

"I'm not a client. Will you find out whether Mr. Bradlock wishes to consult me professionally?"

"He does, of course."

"Well—er—in that case, I have an office too."

Silence.

"And a laboratory, you know. Much more convenient for clients to come here. Not much point in taking the dentist away from the drill, is there?"

"I beg your pardon?"

Gamadge decided to let it go. He scratched a match one-handed on the box, and holding it between two fingers, managed to get a cigarette into his mouth. He lighted the cigarette.

After a pause the voice said briskly: "I'll put Mr. Bradlock on."

"Good."

Gamadge put the match in an ashtray, picked up his pencil, and gently ran it along Martin's head. Martin growled softly. After a minute a masculine voice, pleasant, but showing the effect of long habits of authority, spoke in Gamadge's ear. The voice held a note of perplexity:

"This is Avery Bradlock, Mr. Gamadge."

"Yes, Mr. Bradlock, what can I do for you?"

"I was under the impression—I've just had lunch with a client of mine, an old friend, and in the course of conversation he said—I thought he said that you were— that you went about appraising books and manuscripts, with a view to purchasing, or arranging for sales. There seems to have been an article of yours in the *University Review*—"

"I can see how the error has arisen, Mr. Bradlock. Quite natural, my article may have sounded that way. I'm not a dealer, though, and I'm not qualified to appraise libraries."

"You're not?"

Bradlock sounded so unconvinced that Gamadge laughed. "I know that dealers don't always own up to their profession, but this time it's really true. Anybody in the trade will tell you."

"I must confess that I don't know a thing about it, Mr. Gamadge. I'm so ignorant on the subject that—as you see—I don't even know how to approach it." He laughed too.

"People don't ask me to look at books or manuscripts," said Gamadge, "unless they think something's wrong with them. That's why I have a laboratory—so that I can find out."

"But you must know a great deal about the subject,

and this article of yours—my friend was impressed. He seemed to think you'd be the very person."

"The very person for what, Mr. Bradlock?"

"To look at my brother's papers; that is, unless—perhaps you could tell me: my friend says he knows of a case when a celebrity's correspondence was sold to a collector, sight unseen, for a thousand dollars. Can that be true?"

"It could happen, yes. It wouldn't be extraordinary, if the correspondence was likely to be very interesting, or historically important, or something of the kind."

"It seems incredible."

"Well, the purchaser of such a collection would have a pretty good idea of what he was likely to get." Gamadge, filled with curiosity, asked: "Did you say these papers were your brother's, Mr. Bradlock?"

"Yes. Paul Bradlock."

Gamadge, dumbfounded, sat up in his chair. He had never known that Paul Bradlock was connected with Avery Bradlock of the firm of Ferris, Bradlock and Charles; but then he had never known anything about Avery Bradlock, and very little about the late Paul. And he had been in Europe at the time of Paul Bradlock's death, some two years before. But the relationship did seem almost unthinkable. He asked after a pause: "Is your brother's correspondence for sale, then, Mr. Bradlock?"

"Well, if we could get a thousand dollars for it—it belongs to Paul's wife—we'd be very glad indeed to sell it. But could we?" Bradlock added: "I'm assuming that my sister-in-law would approve. I'm sure she would. I understand"—he hesitated—"my friend seemed to think that such letters couldn't be published without the consent of the writers?"

"They couldn't."

"That of course makes all the difference. What I had in mind was a sale to a collector through some dealer, the usual thing, after somebody had looked the letters over and given us some idea of their value. I was very much afraid it wouldn't be great. My friend said modern autographs don't bring much money. But if we could sell the whole correspondence—do you think we have a chance, Mr. Gamadge?"

Gamadge said: "Impossible to tell. It's all a question of finding your purchaser. Might take years. But if the collection is intact"—Gamadge, recalling what he did know of Paul Bradlock, his life, works and death, proceeded carefully—"people are greatly interested always in the lives of literary men. No, I can easily imagine somebody paying a thousand dollars. Association value, literary history, all that kind of thing."

Bradlock said: "My sister-in-law has of course seen the papers. She used them in writing my brother's life. It came out not so long ago. Most intelligent woman. But the book didn't make money for her—in fact, it lost money. The publisher said that was normal." He laughed.

"Well, I should have thought it would sell. But you can't tell about such things," said Gamadge, reflecting that official lives could be horribly dull, no matter who the subject.

"We liked it," said Bradlock, a little dryly. "Hastily done, of course; but we didn't want other people doing it. We went to his own publishers—he'd had only a play published of late years, you know—and Mr. Meriden was very kind. Brought the book out in a hurry, and he warned us it wouldn't—but never mind that. The important thing is that my sister-in-law should get full value for her property. I know nothing about such things, as I said, but to-day when this man told me about you at lunch, I really thought I'd found the right person to look at those letters."

Gamadge said after a pause: "I could give you some idea of what they might bring in the regular market. I don't think I'd miss anything of special value. These are not your brother's own letters, are they? Or did his wife manage to get hold of any considerable number of them for her book, and will the owners let her have them to sell?"

"I don't know, I don't know at all; I mean I don't know whether she has any of Paul's. She didn't use them. I've never seen the collection—not the kind of thing I understand. I'm very glad indeed that you'll look at it, Mr. Gamadge. I'm quite sure we can trust your judgement. I must consult Vera, of course; speak to her as soon as I get home. As I said, I never had an idea that the papers could be worth anything considerable until Williamson suggested it at lunch."

"I wouldn't take the job on professionally, you know, Mr. Bradlock—not being really qualified. It would be just my opinion, you ought to check on it afterwards."

"Quite out of the question," protested Bradlock, all his instincts offended.

"I mustn't set up as an expert out of my own line, you know. You'd understand that point of view, Mr. Bradlock."

Gamadge could see Bradlock's somewhat amused reaction to such a comparison; it showed in his voice when he replied: "At least people in your line of business don't seem to be obliged to stick to the ledger. Or are you an exception, Mr. Gamadge?"

"I shouldn't think so. If your sister-in-law cares to send the letters along, I'll go through them in my own time. Is it a large collection?"

"I really don't know. I haven't seen them. She spoke as if there were a good many letters—when she first offered to do the biography, after my brother's death. This is extremely kind of you, Mr. Gamadge. I'll consult her." Bradlock hesitated again. "It wouldn't be more convenient for you to look through them on the premises? Where you could confer with her? She might prefer it. She lives practically with us, in a studio annex back of our house up town; she and my brother settled there as soon as they came back from Paris in nineteen hundred and thirty. You'd be quiet and private there."

Gamadge thought that in the circumstances he ought to be allowed to dictate his own terms. "I think not," he said. "It may be a long job. If she likes the idea of my examining the correspondence I think she'd better send it along."

"Well, I'll consult her. I'm sure she'll like the suggestion. But your time is valuable, and I must insist—there ought to be some way of getting around those scruples of yours, Mr. Gamadge."

Gamadge laughed. "People are always interested in

literary correspondence, Mr. Bradlock, as I said. Take it that I'm getting my money's worth in a first look at the Paul Bradlock papers."

"Well"—Bradlock's tone was dry again—"something in that. Thank you very much. I'll call you again."

Gamadge put down the receiver. In June of 1945, when Paul Bradlock died, he and the rest of the world were interested in other things than the death of a poet and playwright, no matter how sensational that death. He had missed all the headlines. What did he know? That Paul Bradlock had had an eerie gift of words, that he had written little for years, that his early promise had not been fulfilled—he was a man of the twenties, whose inspiration had seemed to die after he left Paris with the other exiles after the crash in 1929—and that he had died violently. A hold-up, was it? A drunken brawl? Gamadge seemed to remember that Paul Bradlock's last years had been devoted to alcohol.

But there had been a play, and it had had a success of esteem. Too macabre for the general taste.

Gamadge telephoned to a bookstore. They had the Paul Bradlock *Life*, they didn't have the play. It had been in stock, but was out of print.

Gamadge rang for his old coloured servant Theodore, and asked him to take a cab and a note down to the bookstore. When he had gone, grumbling, Gamadge settled back to his work. The fire hissed, Martin stretched and yawned. Once the folding doors were pushed open a little and a much bundled-up child peered in and waved. Gamadge waved back at him. A starched white arm withdrew him into the hall. Gamadge looked through the window on his left, and realized that the rain had stopped and that there was a blue rift in the cloudy sky.

The clock said three when Theodore came back with the thin parcel. A nice-looking little book, conservatively bound. Good paper, large type. *Paul Bradlock*, by Vera Bradlock.

Gamadge went through it. Paul Bradlock had been born in 1899, had been a brilliant child and a wonderful boy, had gone to Paris to write in the early twenties, had written poetry there and published a volume of verse there: *Spirals*. It was part of a movement, of a literary revolution. Paul Bradlock had evidently been slightly in front of the van—there were long quotations.

He had married Vera Larkin in Paris, another expatriate. Long account here of café life on the Left Bank, nothing that could not be found elsewhere, better done; for the personalities and anecdotes were common property now and if Paul Bradlock had had a private life among friends of his own the *Life* didn't say so.

He had been a charming, gifted, elvish spirit according to Mrs. Paul Bradlock, and when he had been forced home for the usual reason of financial pressure in 1930 he had adjusted himself to his changed surroundings by abandoning his muse and writing plays. One of them, *Getting Out*, had been produced in New York in 1937 for a short run, and afterwards published. It had had some critical acclaim, according to Mrs. Bradlock, but—reading between the lines—Gamadge inferred that it had been too queer to live. He had some faint memory of a revival since Bradlock's death.

According to Mrs. Bradlock, Paul Bradlock had been crushed by discouragement during the war, and had not recovered his spirits by the time he met what she reservedly described as his tragic death. There was a summing up; Paul Bradlock was one of those doomed souls, doomed by an unearthly temperament to frustration and despair. All detail that might have made the *Life* an interesting case history was (understandably) lacking; and all detail that might have made him anything more than a type was suppressed. He might never have had a friend; even his wife seemed nebulous, in the book, as if she had drawn herself from a reflection in a cloudy glass.

Her attempt at a critical appreciation of his work was quite valueless; probably built up from contemporary description of the "movement" in Paris, and from newspaper comment. The style of the book wasn't bad, Mrs. Bradlock was evidently an educated woman who had read much. But she had written a dull, dry book about a man who deserved a little better of her, even if she did overrate his talent, and perhaps his character.

No wonder the publishers, Meriden & Co., had warned the Bradlocks that this family manifesto wouldn't sell.

Gamadge picked up the telephone and called his friend Malcolm.

"Dave? Look here, you're a poet and you lived in France. Do you know anything about Paul Bradlock? . . . I know, you're another generation entirely and years younger, you probably got to Paris after he left. But I thought you might . . . Just a fading memory, was he? Well, come down and tell me what you do remember. And do you know whether his book of poems was ever published in this country? . . . Wasn't? Never mind then . . . Oh, you saw his play? Good. Come on down and bring Ena."

Malcolm said that his wife wasn't in, but that he himself would come as soon as he got his piece written. He was employed on a magazine.

As Gamadge put down the receiver, the front doorbell rang. Martin, always interested in the outer world, started and raised his head.

Since the Gamadges had no reception room on the first floor, it was Gamadge's custom in such circumstances as these to retreat into the laboratory, until Theodore should come and tell him whether the caller was for him, and if so who it was. But it was getting late in the afternoon and Gamadge expected no one. He did not move. Theodore opened the folding doors after an interval, looked in, gave his employer the reproachful glance of one who has done his duty in vain, and held out a tray with a card on it. A tall and slender woman stood just behind him.

Gamadge could only advance to meet her. She said: "I'm Mrs. Avery Bradlock. Is this Mr. Gamadge?"

"Yes. Do come in."

"I ought to have telephoned, but it really wasn't a matter for telephoning. I just got in the car and came."

"Good."

Theodore retreated, pushing the doors to; Gamadge took Mrs. Bradlock's fur from her, and advanced one of the two comfortable leather chairs. She stood looking at him quietly, with a certain interest. "The truth is, Mr. Gamadge, that my husband telephoned and asked me to come and apologize. He says he's completely bungled the whole thing."

# 2

## Emissary

Gamadge said smiling: "I don't know what's been bungled, I'm sure, Mrs. Bradlock, and I'm not conscious of needing an apology. Do sit down and tell me about it."

He sat opposite her and took out his cigarette case. But she already had hers in her hand, a thin gold one. He lighted her cigarette. She looked about her—at the books and files, the moulded cornice, the dusky engraving over the mantel, the antique bronzes on the mantelshelf. Gamadge looked at her.

In her early forties, perhaps, perfectly dressed and groomed. Not an animated face, in fact a colourless one in every sense, but still beautiful, and Gamadge thought humourless. She had red-brown hair, darker eyes, a high, fastidious nose, a thin, exquisitely curved mouth. She wore make-up sparingly; the texture of her skin was so fine that it would have been a pity to hide it.

She said in her expressionless way: "What a charming room. What a sweet little house."

The laboratory door opened and Clara put her head into the room. She had been developing snapshots, and held one by a corner; she was wearing a high-collared indigo-blue smock, and her hair was a brown cloud about the longish oval of her face.

Her grey eyes met Mrs. Bradlock's, and she said: "I'm so sorry. I didn't know there was a client." She withdrew, closing the door.

Mrs. Bradlock remarked: "*Cinquecento*."

"Well, not without the smock, I'm afraid," said Gamadge. "But I must tell my wife that."

"Oh, was it your wife?"

"She is a bit young for the job."

"She looks just like one of those bystanders in the old masters—a saint or an angel."

"She'll be delighted."

"I'm afraid you'll think I'm as stupid as poor Avery was. He realized it as soon as he'd talked to you on the telephone for a minute, and he instantly made inquiries. The first thing he discovered," said Mrs. Bradlock, smiling at Gamadge, "was that you belong to one of his best clubs."

"I'm glad it was one of his best."

"That little one behind this house that nobody can get into. And you went to his university. And you write. And he put his receptionist on you, and she put the secretary on you, and he ordered you down to his office." She looked at Gamadge almost mournfully.

"But, Mrs. Bradlock"—Gamadge was laughing—"why not? I only wish I had legitimate business reasons for going down to Mr. Bradlock's office. I wish somebody would supply me with them!"

"You mean money to invest? He thinks you don't care about money."

"He must think I'm a fool, then. But surely he can understand that even in my business people don't want money on false pretences."

"Well, he does understand, and that's why he's so anxious for you to be the one to look at those letters." Her face, as she referred to the Paul Bradlock correspondence, expressed a slight distaste for the subject; she might be forgiven for feeling it at the very thought of her talented brother-in-law. "But those men down there," she went on in her deliberate way, "they *are* so stupid."

"Oh, don't say that. No reason why they should ever have heard of me, you know."

"I don't mean that it was Avery's fault; that Mr. Williamson—Avery thinks he knows everything because he's made so much money. But he doesn't know anything except that."

"I think he must be wonderful, myself." Gamadge was amused at Mrs. Bradlock. "He needn't bother with the likes of me. He has other things on his mind."

"Thinking you were a dealer!"

"I might well be. Perhaps my article in the *University Review* sounded as if I were."

"Well, it was all stupid, and Avery wants you to come to dinner."

"Oh, he doesn't have to do that." Gamadge was laughing again.

"And look at those letters," said Mrs. Bradlock simply. "Nobody's seen them except Vera, and she isn't an expert—she can't know their value. She'll be cheated. Mr. Gamadge, could they really be sold to somebody for a thousand dollars?"

The Bradlocks seemed fascinated by this round sum. Gamadge said: "Not much chance that they're worth a fraction of it, but collectors do love to pick a correspondence over, and if none of them has ever been published, that boosts the value. Your sister-in-law didn't use many of them."

"Oh, you've read her book? She said people were so scattered, the letters go back so far, and it would have been so hard to get the permissions. I thought it was a very dull book, didn't you? Avery had to pay for it."

"That's quite a usual arrangement, if a family wants a book done in a certain way."

"We had to get it done our way. Even Mr. Meriden—such a nice old gentleman—even he wanted a lot of personal stuff about Paul, and we couldn't have allowed it. There was all that awful publicity when he died."

"I was away."

"It was awful. They lived in our studio, you know; Vera lives there still. We could get any amount of money for it now, if we rented it, but of course she had to stay on while she was working on the book, and Avery can't turn her out until she wants to go—if she ever does. She took all the responsibility for Paul, over all those years. So frightful.

And she has no money except what Avery can give her. It would be nice if she could make some out of the letters."

"Why shouldn't she send them to me?"

"Well, if she could meet you—it would make all the difference. She's very jealous of Paul's things. She always sees his dramatic agent herself, and she would hardly let Avery talk to Mr. Meriden, the publisher. But Avery did see the agent and Mr. Meriden, and there's no money in any of Paul's work now. His play was revived after he was killed— we were against that, but the agent thought it might make money, and Avery didn't like to risk losing anything for her. Mr. Cookson—the agent—really, I don't know what these people are made of. Just because Paul died like that—"

"Where have you been, all your life, Mrs. Bradlock?" Gamadge smiled at her.

"Not here." She returned his look seriously. "I come from the South."

"So I had guessed."

"But I've lived here ever since I was married. I like it better here, Mr. Gamadge. Really I do."

"I'm sure you do."

"The revival wasn't a success. I don't know why it should be; I can't imagine anybody liking that play, even if they could understand it. If you could run up tonight for dinner at half past eight, just a business conference, you know?"

"I could, of course."

"Will you? We dine rather late, because Avery likes to get a little bridge at his club after hours. He never gets home till seven or later." She rose. "You *will* come?"

"Thank you very much, Mrs. Bradlock, I'll be there." Facing her, he smiled. "It will be a scramble, you know, going through a correspondence in a couple of hours. I may find it impossible to get any idea of the value of it at all."

"I'm sure Vera has it sorted. It's so good of you. And we'll feel so much better about it if you come to dinner."

"We'll be square." Gamadge spoke solemnly.

She pulled on long white gloves. "I'll tell Vera as soon as I get home. She'll like you—she's intellectual."

"What a compliment."

Gamadge helped her on with her fur jacket and went to the door with her. A small, handsome town car and a chauffeur waited for her at the kerb. He watched it roll away, then closed the door and went upstairs. Martin jumped off the desk and followed him—it was time for tea.

# 3

# Background

David Malcolm had arrived, and was having tea with Clara in front of the library fire; he was a dark young man of medium height, less disillusioned than he liked to appear. A big tawny chow lay beside Clara's chair, and a yellow cat, younger and smaller than Martin, rushed up to greet that ancient and tried to wrestle with him. Martin stood with his eyes shut and his head up out of the way, not interested. The smaller cat fawned on Gamadge.

"Hello, Junior," said Gamadge. "Hello, Dave. I'm asked out to dinner, Clara. You're not. Mrs. Avery Bradlock thinks you're *cinquecento* and an angelic bystander, but she didn't invite you to dinner. No stray wives for the Bradlocks. It's a business conference."

He sat down and Clara passed him a cup. She said: "Then Mrs. Bradlock and I are even, because I wouldn't ask her to dinner if I could get out of it, either."

"Didn't care for her?"

"She looks so half-alive."

"Not at all, quite a conversationalist. Cultivated, too, if not too bright."

"What's it all about?" asked Malcolm.

Gamadge explained. "So I thought I'd like to know something about Paul Bradlock," he ended. "His wife's book isn't informative. It has some of his poetry in it, though; the kind that has no syntax . . . Take it or leave it, and the reader be damned. Tell me about the play."

"I saw it too," said Clara.

"No, did you?"

"It was quite haunting, didn't you think so, Dave? But I didn't know what it meant."

"What was it *about*?" asked Gamadge.

"Well, there were all these people in an empty room—"

"Empty house," said Malcolm. "The whole house was empty, we were told so."

"But we only saw one room. Really empty, you know," explained Clara. "Perfectly bare."

"And no complaints from the management," suggested Gamadge.

"It was in blank verse," said Malcolm. "Good, too. You learned that there'd been some sort of catastrophe in the neighbourhood—what was it, Clara? Flood? Landslide? Earthquake?"

"I don't think that was explained. But these people couldn't get out without being killed—drowned or buried or . . ."

"Or they'd fall off a cliff," said Malcolm. "They all got out."

"Did they?" Gamadge looked up from his preoccupation with buttered toast.

"One after another," said Malcolm, "and in different ways. Through the door, through the windows, through the cellar, through a trap in the roof. They each had their own reasons for going, and like Clara I rather lost myself in the symbolism. But I suppose the room was reality."

"America in the thirties," said Gamadge, "after Paris in the Golden Age. Paul Bradlock got out all right."

"Got out," added Malcolm, "long before he was killed."

"What do you mean, Dave?" asked Clara.

"He took to drink. Moral tale. *Don't care* came to a bad end."

"It isn't a moral tale just because he was killed in the park," said Clara. "Anybody can get killed in the park if they walk there in the middle of the night."

"But perhaps if he'd been sober he would only have

been knocked out," answered Malcolm. "He probably put up a fight. He was a hopeless alcoholic by that time."

"What made him one?"

"Now you're asking."

"But don't they say there's always some reason?"

"They say lots of things," said Gamadge. "They don't know what to say. Bradlock had talent, but he only published one book of poetry and one play, in all his forty-six years. That might be a reason. He had to leave Paris, where he wanted to be, and come back to America and live on his brother's charity. That might be a reason. But people take to drink who have no such reasons, and sometimes there doesn't seem to be any reason at all."

"I think his fate is implicit in his work," said Malcolm, "if you can judge by his play. He had a brutal point of view, quite sinister."

"Perhaps his wife is right, then, after all," said Gamadge, "and he didn't belong in this world. But not because he was too good for it."

"You still have these illusions about our globe?" asked Malcolm.

"I still have them."

"Well, if you really want to know something about his life—"

"His life in Paris in the twenties," amended Gamadge. "It ought to have been interesting. According to his wife it was pretty dull."

"Dull? Dull?" Malcolm stared. "With all the excitement on the Left Bank, and all the gifted expatriates founding papers and writing manifestoes, and everybody in the cafés talking all night? And he was a young man then. It was all long before my day, the whole bunch of them had run out of supplies and died or gone home, but I kept hearing about it all, I can tell you! Ten years later!"

"Well, Bradlock's wife gives you nothing of it, nothing you can't get from better books. That's one reason I'd like to see those letters, his wife may not have had the sense to know what people would like to read about."

"There may be too much in the letters that people would like to read about," said Malcolm. "If she's protecting his memory she wouldn't publish Paul's high jinks in Paris. But if you're interested I might get some information for you through Pierre Lazo. He's here in New York, and he's an older man—he must have known all about those goings on in the twenties over there. He was a newspaper man— he's here in the International Book Service."

"Do that, Dave, will you?"

"I'll call him tonight. Clara can come up and have dinner with us, since the Bradlocks won't have her, and you can pick her up on your way home. Better take your car, Gamadge; that card of Mrs. Bradlock's says they live up in the Eighties, and if it rains—as I suppose it will—you'll never get a cab up there."

"I've been around," replied Gamadge coldly.

Clara said: "It's very nice of you to ask me, Dave. I've been thinking—what a frightful thing for these Avery Bradlocks; to have all that going on practically in their own house all those years, and then that thing in the park."

"Not at all the kind of people to take it in their stride," said Gamadge. "I feel rather sorry for them."

At twenty-five minutes past eight he drove his car slowly into the Bradlocks' street, on a quiet block of private houses between Madison Avenue and Fifth. The rain was holding off, the sky misty and tinted with rose. There was a fresh, leafy smell in the air—the smell of Spring.

A big modern apartment house on the Madison Avenue corner was cut off from the Bradlock premises by a deep service alley, and a high retaining wall topped by an iron fence. Beyond this was the Bradlock side yard, on street level; it was entered from the street through high iron gates. The yard was turfed and flagged, and set out with shrubs in huge Mexican pots. It led to a little plain square house, almost hidden by the Bradlocks' big one, to which it was joined by a connecting way.

The Bradlock house was a double brown-stone, plain and handsome, with a bow window overlooking the side yard. Gamadge thought that the Bradlock property had probably at one time extended to the corner of the street, and that the little studio annex occupied what had once been the back garden.

He parked his car behind another smaller one, and walked back to the Bradlock front steps. They were low and broad, and the vestibule had a grille. He went in and rang; a parlourmaid admitted him to a well-proportioned hall, took his hat and coat, and ushered him into a large room on the right, which seemed to contain a good many people. But there were only five, and one of them—Mrs. Avery Bradlock, in severe black—left the group and came forward to greet him.

She looked younger in evening clothes and with her head bare, younger and quite beautiful. With her white skin, long slender hands, cold reticence, she might, so Gamadge thought, be the subject of an old song. The proud lady, with who knew what oceans of sentiment concealed under that cold look? Well concealed!

A tall, blonde, ruddy man came up behind her, and was shaking hands with Gamadge even before Mrs. Bradlock had introduced him as her husband.

"Mr. Gamadge, this is really very good of you."

"Not at all," said Gamadge, "I'm delighted."

"I don't know whether we dare"—he looked at his wife, and Gamadge was sure he never did look at her without that expression of pride and love—"do we dare tell him, Nannie?"

"We'll have to."

"Perhaps if we do, he'll go. We can't face that!"

Gamadge said that they couldn't get rid of him now. "For one thing, I'm too hungry."

"Then we'd better confess and get it over with." Bradlock laughed. "You're here on false pretences after all."

"Really?"

"My sister-in-law has sold them. Sold the letters."

"No!"

"As soon as my wife rang her about what Williamson had said—about selling a correspondence *en masse*, you know, sight unseen—Vera got hold of a friend of hers and Paul's—Mr. Iverson, there he is—and he jumped at the chance. He didn't know they were in the market; but of course they weren't until now."

"We all know him," said Mrs. Bradlock. "And the best of it is, Vera got her price."

"The thousand?"

"Yes. You must meet them. But first I want to introduce you to my mother."

An elderly lady, smartly dressed in black lace, took a cocktail from a passing tray and then turned to acknowledge the introduction.

"My mother, Mrs. Longridge," said Mrs. Bradlock. "Mr. Gamadge."

Mrs. Longridge had preserved her figure, and she still showed that she had been a pretty woman in her youth. Her daughter seemed to have inherited nothing from her physically except that short, high, fastidious nose. She said: "They say you're a writer, Mr. Gamadge, and all kinds of interestin' things. I won't be able to talk to you at all. You'll be so bored."

"You talk, Mrs. Longridge," said Gamadge, "and I'll promise to listen."

Mrs. Longridge was delighted. "Makes me feel homesick," she declared, "just to hear a man say a thing like that."

"Well, he mustn't say any more things like that just now," said her daughter. "He must meet Vera and Mr. Iverson."

Mrs. Longridge took a sip of her cocktail. Her face showed entire lack of interest in Mrs. Paul Bradlock and in Iverson; they had probably never bothered to make her feel homesick. Gamadge followed his hostess across the room to the couple who stood talking together at one end of the fireplace. They looked up, cocktail glasses in hand.

"My sister-in-law, Mrs. Paul Bradlock," said Mrs. Avery Bradlock. "And Mr. Iverson. Mr. Gamadge, who so kindly said he'd look at the letters, Vera."

"I know," said Mrs. Paul Bradlock. "It was awfully nice of you, Mr. Gamadge. I'm glad Hill Iverson saved you the trouble. Wasn't it lucky?"

"The luck," said Iverson, "was all mine. Have a cocktail."

The tray was at Gamadge's elbow. He took a cocktail and a little sausage on a stick, and faced the others smiling.

# 4

# Down Payment

Mrs. Paul Bradlock was a small, very blonde woman; small boned, small featured, with a small, clear voice. She was one of those pale blondes whose colouring seems to acquire a kind of dinginess after early youth. If anything can be done to combat this effect, Mrs. Paul Bradlock had not done it—her hair, smooth and loosely knotted, was faded; her light eyes were without sparkle; her skin was without life.

She was almost shabby. Her mauve dress looked as though it might have been made in one piece and belted in—it too had a faded look. But compared with her sister-in-law she was animated. She smiled at Gamadge with lips that were unacquainted with lipstick, and talked steadily and quite gaily.

"They were so afraid you wouldn't come, they refused to let you know!"

"That you'd disposed of your property, Mrs. Bradlock?" Gamadge smiled from her to Iverson.

"It never entered my head that I could sell letters. I didn't know the rules at all." She laughed. "Hill Iverson thinks I'm a ninny, don't you, Hill? I knew I couldn't *publish* them—not without permission; Mr. Meriden explained that to me when we first talked about Paul's biography. But he never said I could sell them! And I wouldn't put them into an auction, of course, or a public sale. Hill won't do that either. Isn't it wonderful that I remembered hearing him say he sometimes bought such things?"

While the clear little voice went on, Gamadge had from time to time exchanged amused or sympathetic glances with Iverson. He had seen him once before, playing in a bridge tournament; and somebody had said that he had been a stockbroker, good old mercantile family, had retired on pre-crash gains, and went around a lot—an eligible bachelor.

He was apparently in his fifties now, a short sturdily-built man with light hair and prominent blue eyes. The eyelids drooped at their outer corners, the droop corresponding to that of his lips. It gave his full, smooth face a semi-cynical, semi-humorous expression. Gamadge had seen a good many people who looked like Iverson, it was almost a type; but what type? One of the people had been a gambler, one an actor, one a lawyer. At any rate, Iverson by the look of him might very well play first-class bridge and make and save money out of a career on the stock market.

Gamadge asked: "Are you a collector, then, Mr. Iverson?"

"Oh, you couldn't dignify me by any such name as that. Never had what it takes for that." Iverson laughed. "I like a flyer now and then. Sometimes it's a lot of books, somebody's library. Sometime's it's a little stock in a play. Sometimes I get the idea that some new artist is going to make good—I bet on him to the extent of buying a few pictures. Just hobbies. I like the element of chance. These letters"—he cast a patronizing, half-affectionate look at Vera Bradlock—"Vera doesn't think much of them, and Paul's friends were duds, most of them; but one or two—fashions change. You never can tell. Whatever I do with them, there won't be a big splash made in the market." He took another cocktail from the parlourmaid's tray. "Glad Vera called me."

"Great fun to be able to indulge one's curiosity in that way," said Gamadge. "I envy you."

"You don't collect at all, Mr. Gamadge?" Vera Bradlock smiled up at him.

"No, just buy a book now and then with the help and advice of my bookseller. Buy it for keeps."

The maid announced dinner. They all went through an archway into a dining-room that must have run half across the rear of the house. A bronze chandelier with frosted globes hung low above a long table. Gamadge found himself placed between his hostess and Mrs. Paul Bradlock, and found the latter prepared to talk about her husband's work.

"I've read your book," he said, "of course. And some of his poetry."

"Oh, he was so very young then; he wrote his poetry before we had even met. I didn't say what I'm going to say now in my book, people misunderstand so—and I do think his poetry was wonderful. But to a certain extent it was no more than a reflection of all that he was surrounded by in Paris, and so strongly believed in. It didn't have the pure originality of his plays."

Mrs. Paul Bradlock was very glib. Gamadge said respectfully: "I only know *Getting Out.*"

"The critics didn't know what to make of it when it first appeared, ten years ago. They weren't ready for it," said Mrs. Bradlock, her small features pinched with severity. "They said it was Russian, and French, and German!" She laughed bitterly. "It was Paul Bradlock! And they practically ignored the revival last year, because it was so hastily and badly done."

"I agree with you fully about its originality," said Gamadge. "That idea of having the room *completely* empty you know. Shattering."

She looked to him in frowning surprise. "Why, exactly?"

"Well, most playwrights would have left something in the room—rags of the outworn past. But your husband implied that it had always been completely empty, and always would be. Of course that made it a little confusing to me, because such a conception of abstract nothingness didn't quite fit in with the fact that people were there in the flesh, supposedly confronted by a real dilemma, no matter what the allegory."

Confused by a glibness that outmatched her own, and that was at least not derived from newspaper criticism, Mrs. Bradlock was spared a reply by Avery Bradlock. Turning from Mrs. Longridge, he said, smiling:

"My wife's mother has a place down in the deep South, Mr. Gamadge, beautiful old place, full of old things. Lots of old letters. She's beginning to think she may have missed her chance at a fortune."

Old Mrs. Longridge, sitting on her son-in-law's right and next to Iverson, ignored that gentleman's interested expression and spoke to Gamadge across the table: "It's a beautiful old place, but it wouldn't be if Avery hadn't fixed it up for me. It was fallin' down. Plenty of stuff moulderin' away in the attic and cellars now. I wondered if you wouldn't know somebody who'd come down to Longridge and look at the things."

"I could certainly find you somebody, Mrs. Longridge."

Iverson met Gamadge's eye. "How about Ellis?"

"Ellis might."

Mrs. Avery Bradlock said with tempered scepticism: "Would it be worth the trouble?" She looked at her husband. "Or the money?"

Avery Bradlock shook his head. "Only one way to find out, isn't there?"

"Always a chance," said Gamadge, "especially nowadays. In the last few decades people have gone document crazy."

Old Mrs. Longridge said: "There now!"

"I had some friends," Gamadge told her, "who let a university librarian go down into their cellar and look at some old account books, mouse eaten and almost illegible from damp. The man said they were history and paid fifteen dollars apiece for them. But that's just a trifling instance. We mustn't forget the old gentleman who offered his collection of letters to a friend for five hundred pounds; only that was a long time ago."

"What about him?" asked Mrs. Longridge eagerly.

"Well, after his death it brought four thousand, and now, a hundred years later, it's valued at twenty thousand. Values change." He smiled at Iverson. "Don't they?"

Mrs. Longridge gasped: "A hundred thousand dollars? Avery . . ."

"Didn't this old gentleman," asked Mrs. Paul Bradlock dryly, "know what he had?"

"Oh yes," said Gamadge, "he knew it was good. But he

didn't know the market, and he certainly didn't know what a hundred years would do to it."

There was a pause. Then Vera Bradlock said: "Well, I can't wait a hundred years, and I'm more than satisfied with a thousand."

Iverson felt in his breast pocket. "Let's close the deal, Vera, shall we? Plenty of witnesses, and I came prepared." Smiling, he laid a folding cheque-book beside his plate, opened it, and took out a fountain pen. "What day is it?"

"It's the fifth," said old Mrs. Longridge, leaning forward. She was fascinated by these business preparations, and quite a flush had risen to her delicately powdered cheeks.

Iverson wrote, tore out the cheque, and handed it to Vera Bradlock, across the old silver épergne. "There you are, my child, and never mind a receipt. But I think I shall take my box of letters away with me."

"You shall," said Vera. She waved the cheque gently back and forth. "It's ready and waiting."

"Well!" exclaimed old Mrs. Longridge, "that's what I call business!"

"It's not what we call business down town," said Avery Bradlock. He was smiling, but he had a doubtful look. "Down town we'd have somebody—say Mr. Gamadge—go through the papers first, and make an inventory."

"Well, you see," said Vera gaily, "I know Hill. Avery, will you take care of this for me?"

She handed it to her brother-in-law, who looked at it, folded it, and put it away.

"Haven't you a bank account, Vera?" asked Iverson.

"A bank account!" she looked at him, her eyes amused but her face grave. "What should I do with one?"

"Oh, but look here, then, I should have brought cash."

There was a short silence. Then Mrs. Avery Bradlock said coldly: "You needn't worry, Mr. Iverson. Vera will get her money."

"Sorry," laughed Iverson. "I see money's nothing to joke about at the Bradlocks'. Sometimes I forget. To me it's just a medium of barter."

Mrs. Longridge said cheerfully: "I just love it. I wish

some of the men in my family had gone in for writin', then perhaps Mr. Iverson would clear out my cellar and give me a thousand dollars. You know, Mr. Gamadge, often as I was in Paris before the depression, and I tell you we knew plenty of people there, I never once even heard of the Left Bank and all that excitement? Never even heard of it!"

A general laugh seemed to please her. Avery said: "Well, your friends there were out of the excitement, I'm afraid, Mrs. Longridge. Pretty conventional set—at least I found them so."

His wife said quietly to Gamadge: "Paul and my husband—it seems so strange, that they should have been own brothers. Poor wretched Paul."

"Yes. Tragic thing."

"He was so promising—and so wild. I never did know him well, and after they came home they lived to themselves. The studio is quite separate, and their friends were not ours."

"Much more sensible for families not to live on top of one another."

"They brought Hilliard Iverson over now and then. We rather enjoyed him, and he plays such good bridge."

"Excellent company, I imagine."

"I suppose Vera is doing the right thing." As the talk around the table died down, she spoke in a louder voice: "We'll have coffee here, and then Mr. Iverson can go over and look at his new acquisition."

"Sight unseen, sight unseen, you know!" Iverson rubbed his hands. "You forget, that's what makes the value. But I'm dying to get my hands on that box. You must all come over with me and witness delivery."

Dessert came in, a fitting climax to a flawless three-course meal. Gamadge turned back to Mrs. Paul Bradlock. He spoke softly: "You've known Mr. Iverson a long time, Mrs. Bradlock?"

"Yes, indeed. He was so fond of Paul, and awfully good to him. Good to me, too, although"—she laughed, glancing across at Iverson—"that was pure benevolence. I'm not exactly his type, as you may imagine."

Gamadge laughed too. "I can see his type! I'm glad you

can trust him with this correspondence. A lot of people, you'd be surprised to know how many, couldn't be trusted with letters that had—let's say nuisance value, for instance."

She was amused. "Poor Hill! He couldn't blackmail anybody with Paul's letters, even if he wanted to. There's a little controversial matter, as Mr. Meriden the publisher so delicately puts it; Mr. Meriden hoped I'd put that sort of thing in my book." She looked down at her plate. "I wouldn't use anything likely to prejudice people against Paul. He could lose his temper, you know." She smiled at Gamadge.

"Who with blood in them can't, if there's enough provocation?"

"I don't think Avery could. He'd just freeze up and walk away." She added: "I don't think Nannie could."

"What a domestic scene! Two snow images walking off in opposite directions."

"You know," said Mrs. Paul Bradlock, "you're very nice and understanding."

"Glad to convey that impression. Are you staying on here in that little house, Mrs. Bradlock?"

"For a while at least. Now that the book is out I shall have time to look around me. I have a nest egg now." She laughed. "I might be able to buy myself into a business. I have friends in the West. Avery was very good to us, Mr. Gamadge; a whole house to live in all these years, and our bills paid. It wasn't meant to be lived in, you know—the studio annex."

"Wasn't it?"

"It was built for one of Avery's aunts, a real musician. She could practise there, and have her concerts. There's just the music room and a bathroom and a little kitchen and pantry to serve refreshments, only I do all my cooking there, and two little rooms upstairs on the gallery—cloakrooms. They're bedrooms now."

"It sounds very compact."

"It is."

"Regular guest house."

"I'm afraid Avery could rent it for a lot."

Gamadge, served with coffee, drank a little before he answered. Then he said: "I don't think you owe the Avery Bradlocks anything."

Her face looked pallid and drawn in the light of the old frosted globes above the table. She said: "Perhaps not."

"There are so many intangibles in human debits and credits."

"Yes. For instance, there's Aunt Bradlock's concert piano." She gave him that strange, hypocritical smirk of hers, and ran a scale on the tablecloth with short, strong fingers. "I get a lot of fun out of that, all free. But I pay for keeping it in tune."

What had those years, alone with Paul Bradlock, done to his wife? She was a woman who didn't care how she looked, and didn't care what people thought of her. Supported by her conviction that the Bradlocks would put up with her forever, perhaps only because people expected it of them, she went her own way. Gamadge wouldn't have cared for her as a neighbour himself.

# 5

# The Other Place

A few minutes later Mrs. Avery Bradlock rose, everybody rose, and the host went directly to a door at the end of the dining-room. Its companion door, at the other end of a built-in Eastlake sideboard, was partly hidden by an immense painted screen, and led to the service pantry; this one opened on a small lobby.

There were three doors leading out of the lobby, and Avery Bradlock unbolted and opened the farther one. The party went through into a short, low passage way, lighted by a single bracket; Bradlock had turned on the switch from the dining-room.

Mrs. Paul Bradlock passed him, opened a door at the

end of the passage, and stood aside, smiling. She said: "Do come in."

Gamadge and Iverson were last. Gamadge closed the door for Vera Bradlock, and then stood looking around a big, high room. It was two stories high, with a gallery running along the wall on the west, and a narrow wooden stair rising from the south-west corner to the gallery, and up above it to a trap-door in the ceiling.

Vera followed his look. "I have a nice attic," she said. "A splendid air-chamber for the hot weather."

"All the comforts." Iverson, hands in pockets, smiled at the ceiling, which had a damp-stain in the south-east corner, and a large crack running through the stain down the wall.

"Now, Hill!" But her demure expression convinced Gamadge anew that Mrs. Paul Bradlock was a satirist.

The room was inexpressibly dreary. Ornate standard lamps with battered and faded shades lighted up the shabby chintz-covered furniture, the worn old rugs on the worn flooring, the empty hearth strewn with ashes and cigarette ends, the marred top of the open concert-grand piano. There was a typewriter on a table near a window, with papers beside it.

The only brightness in the place came from a gay unframed painting above the bare mantel, perhaps the only memorial of Paul Bradlock's life in Paris.

Mrs. Longridge and the Avery Bradlocks stood together, and there was a kind of horror in their attitude. Bradlock said: "I had no idea."

Mrs. Longridge turned to look at their hostess. "I must say, Vera," she observed with her usual candour, "you need a decorator."

"It's all right," said Vera.

"But I didn't know," protested Avery in a shocked voice, "that it was *damp*."

"Oh, that's nothing. That happens now and then when it rains for a long time. It's been so rainy this Spring," said Vera. "It soon dries out."

"Good God, dries out!" He swung to face her. "How's the plumbing?"

"All right, Avery."

Mrs. Longridge had begun a tour of the room. She stopped now before a low bookshelf, containing a dozen or so books, a pack of cards, some teacups, writing materials, and a broken flowerpot. She said: "Bohemian."

"I'm afraid so," replied Mrs. Paul Bradlock cheerfully. "I haven't much closet space."

Mrs. Longridge went on to the grand piano, drew delicate fingers over rings made by wet tumblers, bent to examine a cigarette burn, and clucked disapprovingly.

A small, thin, pale girl with wispy brown hair and a pink-tipped nose came in from a doorway; she was wiping her hands on a paper towel. She stood unsmiling, gazing at the strangers.

"All right, Sally," said Vera Bradlock. "You can knock off."

The small girl rolled down the sleeves of her sweater, snatched up a coat from a chair, and hurried across the room to the front door. She sidled hastily out, and the door closed behind her.

"My little cousin," said Mrs. Paul Bradlock placidly. "She's been with me since Paul died. Looking for your property, Hill? There it is."

A rough wooden packing-box, perhaps thirty inches long and a foot wide and high, stood labelled and ready under the stairs. "I thought you might want it sent," she explained.

"Not a bit of it. I have my car." Iverson went over and stood looking down at it. He was smiling broadly. "You certainly made a job of it!"

"Oh, Tom Welsh hammered the top on. I've had it up in the attic for years. It was just right."

Gamadge had joined Mrs. Longridge at the piano, which stood near the stairway. He leaned on the scarred top, looking down with interest at the box. "Be heavy, perhaps," he said.

"Oh, Tom will help him," said Mrs. Paul Bradlock.

Iverson turned to her. "You declare this," he said with mock solemnity, "to be the private papers of Paul Bradlock deceased, and you now make them over to me for the sum of one thousand dollars, paid by me in the presence of these witnesses?"

"I do," said Vera.

Mrs. Avery Bradlock had joined the others at the piano. She asked Gamadge faintly: "What must you think of us?"

"Because your studio shows the passage of time?" He smiled. "I sometimes wish they'd let me have some cracks myself, instead of an endless chain of plasterers and painters."

"I should die here."

"You should have been at Longridge, Nannie," said her mother coolly, "before Avery fixed it up for me. You don't remember."

"I remember, Mamma."

"You can't remember much, sent away to school by your Uncle Forester till he lost his money, and travellin' with me till we all lost what was left, and then gettin' married. All you remember about Longridge is ridin' around with your cousins, and all the harness mended with pieces of rope."

"The studio was all right when Paul and Vera came here to live."

"Fifteen and more years ago!"

Mrs. Avery Bradlock glanced about her. Vera Bradlock and Iverson had moved to the fireplace, that communal ashtray, and were standing with their elbows on the shelf, talking and smoking. Avery Bradlock was still contemplating the sprawl of damp on the ceiling at the other end of the room. Mrs. Avery said very low: "You *know* how it was, Mother. They lived their own life here, we weren't welcome; they knew we shouldn't like their parties. And later—in the last few years—nothing would have induced Avery to see Paul. Nobody could come here then."

"I don't like drunken men myself," said Mrs. Longridge. "But if Vera Bradlock—and I don't like her either—if she had the full responsibility for lookin' out for him, you and Avery might have seen to it that she was comfortable."

"Nobody could interfere. You're really being very unfair, Mother."

There was a step on the gallery. Everybody looked up;

a heavy-shouldered dark young man in khaki slacks and shirt had come out of one of the upper doors and leaned on the rail, looking down. His eyes wandered incuriously from one group to the other, and across the room to Avery Bradlock. His narrow face was expressionless.

Vera said: "Oh, Tom; I hope we didn't wake you." She explained at large: "It's Sally's friend, Tom Welsh. He has a temporary night job at a hospital, and he gets his sleep in the daytime."

Mr. Welsh, running a hand over his thick dark hair, mumbled that it was about time for him to get up, anyway.

"And just in time to help me with my box," Iverson told him. "If you'll be so good, Welsh? Help me get it into the back of my car? And how about driving down with me and giving me a hand with it at the other end? My walk-up"—he laughed—"I wouldn't live any other way, but there's a certain lack of service."

Welsh said nothing in reply; but he came down the stairs, dragged the box out from under them, and ignoring Iverson's half-hearted gesture of assistance, heaved the box to his shoulder. He started off with it to the front door, which he opened with his other hand.

"Good heavens," said Iverson, watching him go, "I feel as if I'd wound him up. I'd better catch up with him before he rips the cover off the luggage compartment by main force. I'll just run through and grab my hat and coat." He went from one to the other of the party, shaking hands. "Good-bye all, and thanks for a delightful evening. I can get through, I suppose? No, don't bother. Mr. Bradlock, I'm off. Vera, thank you again."

He waved an arm when he reached the inner door, and disappeared into the connecting passage. The door closed behind him.

"Well!" said Vera after a moment. "That didn't take long. And what"—she smiled at the others—"shall we do now? A little bridge? I don't play, but I'm sure Mr. Gamadge does and I know the rest of you are devoted to it. It's quite early yet."

Gamadge said that it was after ten, and that he was picking his wife up. He'd better be going along too. "It's been a great pleasure, Mrs. Bradlock." He shook hands with Vera. "Quite an event. Glad I was in on it." He turned to his other hostess. "Most enjoyable evening."

Avery Bradlock came up. "Wish you'd stay. We could adjourn to the other house."

"Awfully good of you, but I won't be sorry to get my wife home early. She's been overdoing it."

"I hope very much to meet her soon," said Avery's wife.

Old Mrs. Longridge was evidently preoccupied. She had been gazing thoughtfully at the front door ever since it closed behind Welsh and his burden, and now she asked with interest: "Who *is* that young man, Mrs. Paul?"

"Just a nice boy out of the armed services. He was in the merchant marine, and his ship was sunk. He had a dreadful time. They had him at the Medical and Surgical Hospital for ages, and now they've given him this job as orderly. He's really a chemist, I think, or was going to be." Mrs. Paul offered this information smilingly.

"Well," inquired Mrs. Longridge, "why *ain't* he a chemist then?"

"Because he isn't up to brainwork yet."

"He lives here?"

"Camps here, you might say."

"You certainly have quite a family."

"Haven't I? But housing is so difficult, and Tom Welsh has no money."

Mrs. Longridge moved towards the passage doorway, which her son-in-law held open for her. She said: "You get Avery to fix up this place for you."

"Well, it has to be fixed; but not for me—if I go."

"Go?" Mrs. Longridge gave her a stern look, pausing in her walk to do so. "Who said you were goin'?"

"Nobody," laughed Vera.

"I should think not."

The Bradlocks, Mrs. Longridge and Gamadge went through into the passage. Bradlock fastened the door after him. "Safer for both households," he said. "No use giving sneak thieves a free passage."

"I don't know what's got into you, Mother," said Mrs.

Avery as they all emerged into the dining-room. "Settling Avery's affairs for him like that. And inviting Vera to stay for ever."

Bradlock said: "Of course she can stay for ever if she likes. Why in God's name didn't she tell me the place was falling down on top of her?"

"I never liked her," said Mrs. Longridge, "but I'm beginnin' to think she's a nicer woman that I thought she was."

"Did you know she had all those young people living there with her, Nannie?" Bradlock looked puzzled.

"Of course I didn't."

"I hope they get enough to eat," said Mrs. Longridge. "Your grandfather Longridge used to put up his friends and relations for months, but then we mostly lived off the place."

Mrs. Avery Bradlock smiled at Gamadge. He said good-bye again, and Bradlock got his coat and hat for him and saw him off; they parted amiably, but Bradlock's face still wore its puzzled look.

Gamadge, whose expression was not dissimilar, got into his car and drove down to the apartment in the Seventies where the Malcolms lived. It was on a corner of Lexington Avenue; the doorman was out under the canopy taking the air. He greeted Gamadge as an old friend, and took him up in the elevator.

# 6

# Gamadge Wants to Know

Malcolm opened the door, and stood looking at Gamadge in some surprise. "You're early."

Gamadge walked past him into the bright green-and-silver lobby. He said: "My services weren't required, after all."

"No?" Malcolm closed the door and leaned against it, eyebrows raised, while Gamadge peeled off his coat. "They give you a good dinner?"

"Couldn't have been better. I'm full up but not uncomfortable."

"That's good. Still interested in Paul Bradlock, or did you get what you wanted to know from his family?"

"I'm still interested. Anything for me?" Gamadge dropped his coat and hat on a chair and turned to survey Malcolm alertly.

"Something. I think I can tell you why Mrs. Paul Bradlock didn't have much to say about Bradlock's life among the writers of Paris."

"You can, can you?"

"We might go back to the dining-room. I got a couple over to play bridge, and I'm out this rubber."

They went along the hall, past the sitting-room, where Clara, Elena Malcolm and the "couple" were so engrossed that they didn't even raise their heads. In the little dining-room Gamadge sat down at the round table while Malcolm mixed highballs at a buffet. Gamadge said: "This modernistic stuff of yours—it's very light and bright, I must say."

"What drives you to this handsome admission?"

"I've been wandering in a phantasmagoria. I've seen splendours and miseries, solid old elegance next door to dilapidation. I feel a little confused."

"And a little depressed?" Malcolm looked at him, more and more surprised.

"Not that exactly."

"Let's hear about it." Malcolm brought the tray to the table, and sat down beside his guest.

"After you. Tell me what you dug up."

Malcolm took a scrawled envelope out of his pocket. "Lazo didn't know Bradlock, but he called up a couple of other men that had met him around in cafés. But Bradlock was only there to meet other writers in the movement. His personal friends weren't on the Left Bank; not at all."

"Weren't they?" Gamadge lighted a cigarette.

"If Mrs. Paul Bradlock didn't write about them, it was because they were too dull to write about. The expatriates her husband knew best were the ones that lived in hotels and luxury apartments—I don't think they ran to palaces—on the Right Bank, all among the tidy rich. If some of them lost money after nineteen hundred and twenty-nine they didn't lose pittances, they lost fortunes. They ran *salons*, they gave dinners, they watched the literary revolution from a safe distance and with benevolent detachment. They could always be depended on for a square meal, and I dare say they made good listeners. Some of them were on the fringes of literature themselves. Dilettantes. I have a little list."

"Good."

"That fellow, Stark"—Malcolm pointed with his pencil—"he lives there yet. A survivor. Writes little articles in French for reviews. Mrs. Cobway had a *salon*, took to painting. I think she's in Italy now; I heard of her myself now and then, a confirmed Florentine. This Jeremy Wakes was a man of family, travelled, spent time in England, where he knew a lot of well-placed people, but had his headquarters in Paris. He wrote little books about curiosities of literature and that kind of thing, they've been published over here. Lazo says one met him everywhere.

"His wife was also of good family, and she came up with one pretty good book, a biography of a French eighteenth-century writer; or was it a collection of short lives? Meriden published her. Wakes died in Paris in the thirties, she came back to America.

"This Toller, a fashionable doctor, killed himself after the crash. He used to have literary evenings, went in for foreign nobility, the kind that write memoirs.

"Here's another fatality—man called Brandon. A scholarly old person, a diner-out. After nineteen hundred and twenty-nine he shot himself.

"Well, that's all Lazo got." Malcolm shoved the envelope to Gamadge. "And you can see that the list wouldn't show up very brilliantly in Bradlock's *Life*. Nonentities, they wouldn't do anything to explain Paul Bradlock's curious charm."

"No. Thanks, Dave." Gamadge put the envelope away.

"If I'd had this it might have helped me with Mrs. Paul at dinner."

"Lazo says his friends say she was an uninteresting little person in a bookshop, pretty but without much charm. What did you think of her?"

"Not pretty, no charm."

"Lazo says she came to Paris in her teens, one of the horde that wanted a look at the earthly paradise; but she actually did have a job, and went on with it after she and Bradlock married. But it wasn't enough to support them both after Bradlock's remittances ceased. They had to go back home. Now tell me what happened tonight. Did they decide against selling the papers?"

Gamadge told him. When he had finished, Malcolm sat looking at him thoughtfully; there was a long silence. At last Malcolm said: "Funny business. Funny set-up, too."

"Funny any way you look at it."

"You think this Iverson's getting away with something?"

"Whether he is or not, something stands out a mile." Gamadge looked up. "You see it, don't you?"

"According to you, even Avery Bradlock was uneasy about the circumstances of the sale to Iverson; but he was the one who suggested that kind of sale in the first place, and you back him up on it. You said such things were done."

"They have been. But the thing that impresses me is the ungodly hurry of it. Look at the timetable.

"Those papers have been lying around for two years, the widow didn't know they had any commercial value. This afternoon, as soon as Avery Bradlock hears from a friend that such papers have or may have value, he calls me and verifies the information; he verifies the fact that collectors have paid as much as a thousand dollars for a first go at a literary correspondence.

"He calls his wife immediately; say at half past two o'clock. Mrs. Avery rings her sister-in-law—rings her, mind you, the Avery Bradlocks don't call at the studio. Between a quarter to three and seven—when Bradlock gets home—in less than four hours, presumably a good deal less, Mrs.

Paul Bradlock has found a buyer. The thousand dollars are paid down two hours later, and the box of papers, crated up and labelled, are out of the place an hour after that. And," finished Gamadge, "I don't have to see the papers at all."

Malcolm drank some of his highball, put down the glass, and looked at it. He said: "The thing's plausible. She knew Iverson, they all knew him, and he knew Paul Bradlock. He'd have some idea what the correspondence would consist of. He agrees to keep it out of the open market. He's willing to pay the exact price mentioned, certainly a fair price, and he's interested in such things and a friend of Mrs. Paul's."

"Plausible, yes. Avery Bradlock couldn't protest," said Gamadge. "Even I couldn't. But the fact is there: as soon as there is any question of those papers being examined by anybody, they're out of circulation, in a nailed box, sold and practically delivered. They're nailed up out of sight before I arrive. Iverson brings his cheque book, and hauls them off with him. That thousand dollar cheque blocked Avery Bradlock; he couldn't resist it. It simply dazzled him. A thousand dollars for a lot of letters!"

"And of course they were his sister-in-law's property. *She* was probably dazzled, too. Again I ask—is Iverson getting away with something?"

"You don't get it at all," said Gamadge irritably. "She and Iverson were in the deal together. It sticks out a mile. She's not a fool, and she assured me that she knew what she was doing. I'm sure she did. You know, Malcolm"— Gamadge half closed his eyes—"I can't convey it, but it was obvious that they were enjoying themselves over it; it was a game. She wouldn't have let anybody block it."

"Well, then, what game? That doesn't make sense, Gamadge. If they're worth more than a thousand, why should she cheat herself? No reason why she should conceal their value from Avery Bradlock; or"—Malcolm glanced up—"would there be? There's an idea, and a pleasant one, I must say! These people were living on him, and he must have had all kinds of expenses in connection with Paul Bradlock's death, and there was that *Life* he paid for. Would he try to repay himself out of what she made from those letters? Is that why she handed him that cheque in that cynical way?"

Gamadge shook his head. "He's not like that. If he were, he'd have made the devil's own fuss about that kind of sale to Iverson. He'd never have suggested such a thing in the first place." Gamadge thought it over, and shook his head again. "He wanted her to get the money."

"Well, then it can't be that the papers were worth more than a thousand."

Gamadge asked slowly: "What if they were worth less?"

"Less?"

"What if they were worth nothing?"

Malcolm stared. "I don't—"

"What if they were non-existent?" Gamadge laughed. "Don't look so blank; that might explain everything."

"How?"

"Well, look at it; after Paul Bradlock's death his penniless widow sells every saleable thing he owned, as she had a perfect right to do. That studio annex was as bare as the palm of your hand, except for broken-down worn-out stuff that evidently belonged there, and a painting that had nothing to recommend it but colour—so far as I could judge—and probably would bring nothing. She may have sold through Iverson; that character—there are mighty few games he wouldn't play, unless I'm mistaken. But she'd mentioned letters to her brother-in-law Avery—in connection with her book. However, she has no reason to think that Avery will feel any future interest in them; they're not his property in the first place, and he doesn't know or care anything about such things. He's a busy man, with lots of ways to occupy his time, and my impression is that the less he has to think about his brother Paul, the better he'll be pleased.

"But suddenly a pal of Bradlock's, somebody whose opinions carry weight with him, informs him that a correspondence of that kind often has a commercial value. Then Bradlock *is* interested. Through his wife he springs the news on Mrs. Paul. Well, that's awkward for her, isn't it?"

"You mean he wouldn't like to find out that she's been

selling stuff and pocketing money on the quiet. But after all—"

"After all, she's living there in her own house, and sheltering a couple of other people, and getting all her living expenses paid, entirely subject to Avery Bradlock's goodwill. There are worse things than cracks in the ceiling, Dave; no wonder she didn't bother her brother-in-law with complaints about cracks in the ceiling! Or bother his wife, either—how about Mrs. Avery's goodwill? There isn't any too much of that lying around at the disposal of Paul Bradlock's widow. If Mrs. Paul moved out it would certainly be into a very small place, and if she lost Avery's goodwill she'd probably lose all but a bare living. He struck me as a very decent sort of man, but he's the sort to be rather disgusted by what looked like sharp practise of any kind."

"So you think she and Iverson got up this charade tonight to conceal the fact that she'd sold those letters?" Malcolm smiled. "If you thought that at the time, it must have been slightly irritating to watch. There you were, perfectly helpless, while Iverson and the lady did it all with mirrors."

"I'm pretty sure of one thing, anyway," said Gamadge. "She's where she is because Bradlock's sense of duty—and perhaps his respect for public opinion—keeps her there. But if he found out that she'd sold his brother's papers on the sly, while he paid for the cost of publishing that biography, I think she'd move into a furnished room. They could let that studio for any money now, as I'm sure Mrs. Avery would be the first to remind him." Gamadge took a swallow of whisky, and put down his glass. "Of course I may be entirely wrong about the whole thing; but if it wasn't a charade, as you call it, I shall be surprised."

"You sound as if there were some way of finding out. How can you do that, would you mind telling me? Iverson got the box out from under your nose."

Gamadge looked at him, half smiling. "Care to help me out with a little test?"

"I'd be delighted."

"Perhaps I oughtn't to get you into this. It may be more of a game than it looks. Iverson—" Gamadge fanned cigarette smoke away from his face, frowning. "I don't think he plays any game for love."

"Don't worry about me, Grandpa."

Gamadge felt in his pocket. "I got his address. Mrs. Paul had the box nicely labelled, and I got a look at the label. Here you are. Address in the East Fifties, and he said it was a walk-up."

Malcolm took the paper, read the address on it, and looked up. "Nice mid-town location. What do I do about it?"

Gamadge leaned forward and talked earnestly. When the bridge four came in for drinks he and Malcolm were laughing.

# 7

# Offensive

At a little after ten o'clock on the following morning David Malcolm stood in the vestibule of a converted private house, pushing a bell marked *Iverson*.

It was a handsome house, whose original owner must have had taste as well as money; a delicate iron balcony ran across the first story front, the superintendent's basement was hedged off from the street by well-kept shrubs, and the vestibule in which Malcolm stood was tiled with lozenges of black and white marble. There seemed to be only four tenants, one to a floor, and by the arrangement of the bells and mailboxes Iverson was apparently one flight up.

The door clicked, and Malcolm went in. He climbed well-carpeted stairs to a narrow landing. A voice asked: "That the cleaner and valet?"

"No, I'm calling on Mr. Iverson."

Iverson himself stood in an open doorway. He was clad in a short brocade dressing-gown over pyjamas, and Malcolm thought that his morning face had a certain coarseness. He looked at his caller inquiringly, and amiably enough; Malcolm was highly presentable.

"Want to see me?" he asked.

Malcolm was a little taller than the man in front of him, and could get a view of part of the large sitting-room over Iverson's shoulder. He got what he could in the moment allowed him—"Might slam me out," he thought, his eyes fastened on a compact mass of newspapers which had been placed on a side table near the door. The papers looked as if they had been moulded into shape by tight packing; they made an oblong that probably measured twelve by twelve by thirty inches.

"I ought to have telephoned," said Malcolm, assuming a timid and apologetic air which was very foreign to his nature. "But I hate explaining over the telephone, and one so often gets no farther than the house man. *Does* one?"

"Well," said Iverson, a little less amiably, "that depends. Doesn't it?"

"It certainly does." Malcolm laughed with genteel diffidence. "I thought I'd just take a chance. I *am* so interested in Paul Bradlock. I write a little poetry myself. I'm one of his greatest admirers. My name's Malcolm."

Iverson's expression did not change, not by the flicker of an eyelid. "Just one of those good old outcasts of Poker Flat," thought Malcolm. "Might have dealt faro all his life." But he was inclined to think that the full, pale face swelled a little, and there was certainly a reddening of blood vessels over the cheekbones; perhaps Mr. Iverson's only way of flushing.

Iverson moved a little to the left, cutting off Malcolm's view of the newspapers on the side table. He said: "I don't know who can have given you my name, Mr. Malcolm."

"Oh, I ought to have said. Mr. Gamadge did—Henry Gamadge, you know, the criminologist."

"The what?" Iverson's face was still blank, but his voice flattened.

"The criminologist, you know."

"I don't know. I understood that Mr. Gamadge was a— if anything, a graphologist."

"Oh, he is; but he's very good at crime, too. He found

out who murdered a stepmother of mine," said Malcolm
earnestly. "If he hadn't, I might have been hanged myself.
That's how I know that he's a criminologist. He doesn't talk
about it."

"Evidently not." Iverson surveyed Malcolm with rising doubt. "Are you serious?"

"You can look it up."

"I'll take your word for it. What about Paul Bradlock?"

"Well, I did hope that I might get just a look at those
papers before you dispersed them."

Iverson said: "I'm surprised that Mr. Gamadge mentioned the papers to anyone. It was a private transaction—I
thought he understood that. He wasn't even in on it
professionally; he definitely told Avery Bradlock that he
wasn't an expert in that line at all, he wouldn't even look at
the letters professionally."

"That's so, he only goes in for disputed documents. But
of course he was greatly interested, and he thought that
after you'd had a first whack at the letters you might let me
have a look too—at your convenience, and of course in the
most confidential way. There ought to be a lot of juice in
them," said Malcolm eagerly. "Lots of controversy. Paul
Bradlock was such a fighter."

"The papers are not on view," said Iverson, his hand
now on the door-knob, "and they may never be. And if you
want my frank opinion of Mr. Gamadge's behaviour in
sending you here, Mr. Malcolm, I'll tell you—it was
damned officious of him."

The sudden ferocity in Iverson's voice seemed to
intimidate his caller. Malcolm backed away a little. "Oh, he
didn't send me—don't blame him, Mr. Iverson! *We* were
just talking, because he knew I was such a Bradlock fan.
Just talking at the cigar store, after breakfast. I came right
down. I'm awfully sorry."

Iverson said with icy repression: "If I ever show any of
the Bradlock correspondence it will be to fellow collectors
of my own choosing. It isn't even unpacked yet, and I'm
taking it out of town with me to explore at my leisure."

"Of course." Malcolm took another backward step.

"Surely you understand, Mr. Malcolm"—Iverson's

voice softened, and he smiled—"that the less known about such collections, the greater their value in the collectors' world. I shouldn't have dreamed of buying this one if Mrs. Paul Bradlock had used any of it in her life of her husband, for instance."

"I understand perfectly." Malcolm looked over his shoulder at the stairs as if he would have liked to make a dash for them.

Iverson seemed to regret his former annoyance. "Wish I could ask you in to have a little talk about Paul, but the place is a mess. The woman hasn't been up yet."

"Oh, thanks, no, that's all right. I'm awfully sorry. Please overlook the intrusion. My fault." Malcolm sounded faintly hurt. "Good morning. I should have telephoned, I know."

"Sorry not to be able to accommodate you." Iverson, smiling frostily, closed the door.

Malcolm ran down the stairs, out to the street, and down the area steps behind the row of shrubs. He rang at the grille. A woman in working clothes came and looked out at him.

He said: "This the superintendent?"

"Me husband is next door just now, sir."

"Oh, well; I've just been up calling on Mr. Iverson. He said there was a wooden box sent down, and I wondered if I could have it. I hate cartons," said Malcolm, taking a dollar bill out of his wallet. "Especially for packing china, and you know how hard packing-crates are to get hold of. Could you help me out?"

The woman said: "Well now, sir, I believe there is a box. I'll get it for you. Me husband hasn't it broke up yet, I'm pretty sure of that."

"Thank you so much. I'll just see if I can hail a cab."

Malcolm had the cab at the kerb before the superintendent's wife came out with the box. It was in fine condition, with the cover loosely attached by its nails. Malcolm pressed the dollar into her hand.

"Tell Mr. Iverson I got it all right, will you?"

"I'll be going up any minute to do his rooms."

Malcolm got himself and the box into the cab and drove away.

Ten minutes later it was on Gamadge's laboratory table, and he and Malcolm stood contemplating it lovingly.

"And the beauty of it is," said Malcolm, "that there needn't have been a box, all we needed was for Iverson to know I asked for it. But there it is. Is it the right one?"

"I could swear to it," Gamadge inspected it. "He tore the label off, the sly dog—thought he was cutting communications. What an ass he is. That's always the trouble with these twisters, they have such bad consciences they overdo everything. Why shouldn't the superintendent see a box with Mrs. Paul Bradlock's writing on it?"

"And then he goes and leaves those newspapers just as they were when he unpacked them, and right in line with the doorway."

"He didn't expect you."

"Poor Iverson, such self-control, and then the delayed shock coming out in that exhibition of fury. Pitiful. He got himself together pretty fast, though."

"He did everything wrong. If he'd been on the level he needn't have wasted any time on you at all; the normal thing would have been to say he was sorry, nothing doing, and politely shut the door in your face. But he had to know what you were up to."

"I'll tell you another funny thing. After I told him you were a crime man, and he'd recovered from that, he asked me what about Paul Bradlock. Not Paul Bradlock's letters, but Paul Bradlock." Malcolm looked at Gamadge thoughtfully. "Am I wrong? I thought that was rather odd."

"It's odd. It means that the letters weren't on his mind because there were none, but that Paul Bradlock is."

"Oh well, natural enough, perhaps, with all my talk about him. What'll he do now?"

"He'll wonder whether I'm going to spill all this to the Avery Bradlocks, and why. He can't get around that lie he told you about not having unpacked the letters."

Malcolm, sitting on the edge of the table, looked inquiring. "Well, what are you going to do? Or was this test carried out purely in the interests of scientific truth?"

Gamadge did not answer directly. He stood with his hands in his pockets, staring down at the box and scowling.

After a pause he said: "She left all those people out of her book."

"For heaven's sake, we've been over that."

"You have. *I* didn't say she left them out because they were dull. I wish—" Gamadge took Malcolm's list out of his pocket. "I wish we could find some of them. Let's see. Wakes, Toller and Brandon are dead. Stark is in Paris. Mrs. Cobway—you think—is still living in Italy. How about Mrs. Wakes? You say she came back to America."

"At least ten years ago. She may be anywhere now— may have gone back to Europe and been lost in the war. Why are you bothering about her or any of them?"

"They're Paul Bradlock's past, and his wife suppressed it. She suppressed whatever correspondence he did leave, and she's played a very queer game about it with Iverson. Looked tough to you, too, did he?"

"You should have seen him when I mentioned your hobby."

"Guilty conscience, all right. Do me the favour to remember that this skulduggery about the letters wasn't a crime. He has something on his mind besides that."

"If you told the Bradlocks, you might get Mrs. Paul thrown out of her studio. You thought so yourself." Malcolm frowned at his friend.

"Iverson doesn't know me; perhaps he does believe that I'm the kind of poisonous busybody who'd do that—for any such reason."

Malcolm laughed. "After this morning, I don't know why he shouldn't believe anything."

"In any case, I think we'll hear from him." Gamadge was fingering a corner of the packing-box, raising the lid a little and pressing it down again. He said: "We'd have heard from him already, but he has to consult his partner."

Malcolm rose. Turning his hat in his hands, still frowning at Gamadge, he said: "You say you don't want to make trouble for her, but you still seem bent on turning up her past."

"That needn't make trouble for her." Gamadge looked up at him. "I assumed that I didn't have to swear *you* to secrecy."

"No, you didn't. Just keep me posted, will you? I'm interested myself."

When Malcolm had gone, Gamadge made two appointments by telephone. Then he went up and told Clara that he was going out on business and didn't think he'd be back until late afternoon. He went out, walked to a subway, and rode down town.

# 8

# Research

At a quarter to twelve Gamadge was sitting in a small office, looking across a flat-topped desk at Detective-lieutenant Durfee. Gamadge sat slumped down in his hard chair, legs stretched out and lighted cigarette dangling from limp fingers. Durfee had some papers in front of him.

"Didn't you read the newspapers?" asked Durfee.

"I was out of the country at the time. Now I'm doing a little research on Paul Bradlock, and I thought you might have something the papers never got."

"Not much of anything," said Durfee. He consulted the file. "Twelfth of June, nineteen hundred and forty-five. It wasn't a mugging, somebody beat his head in. He was having a walk sometime after midnight—not long after midnight—in Central Park. It was either a hold-up—his pockets were turned out—or a brawl with a bar crony, which he often indulged in towards the end of the evening. The crony might not have robbed the body to fool us, he might have needed the money. Bradlock was always broke himself." Durfee looked up. "You know that part of the park up there, around the Reservoir?"

"I was brought up around the Reservoir."

"Then you know that entrance from Fifth Avenue up above Eighty-fifth Street. You go in and there are two walks, one straight ahead and one up some steps. That one goes along parallel to the Reservoir, but down below it, this side of the drive. There's a slope down to the Fifth Avenue wall, which is very high along there, and even with the bottom of the slope. The walk has benches along it on the Fifth Avenue side, and a three-bar railing, and lots of trees and shrubbery. Very dark at night, if you get between the lights. This was a rainy night, too, and there wasn't anybody in the vicinity.

"Bradlock wasn't found by park keepers or a policeman. He wasn't found till early next morning, about eight o'clock. A passer-by on Fifth Avenue noticed one of his feet showing out from behind a bush just beyond the top of that high wall. He'd been killed on the walk, or so we imagine, his body hoisted over the rail or pushed through between the bars—he was a small, slight man, and very thin—and rolled down. You going to put all that in your piece?"

"I might use some of it. People like details of the lives of the poets."

"They certainly did at the time. Boy! I was sorry for the family."

Gamadge took a pull at his cigarette. Then he asked: "Which theory do the police like best—hold-up or brawl?"

"It's fifty-fifty. Here's the argument back and forth; a pro doesn't go out of his way to kill a drunk, but a drunk mightn't have any more sense than to put up a fight; in which case the poor pro might actually have to kill him in self-defence."

"And the bar crony, on the other hand, wouldn't be so likely to have a weapon. You can't beat a man's head in with an ordinary walking stick or an umbrella."

"That's so. The weapon could have been a section of steel pipe. Which is in favour of the pro again, because he'd be more likely to use something padded up, like a blackjack or a sandbag."

"But a hold-up man wouldn't be strolling with him in Central Park."

"How do you mean?" asked Durfee.

"Bradlock wasn't on his way home; that section of the park is above the street where he lived. He must have been taking a walk. Why do that on a rainy night, at that hour, unless a friend persuaded him to do it?"

"He was drunk, I tell you. Every night of his life at that hour he was staggering drunk. He could have gone any place. He often did. He'd been found in the park before, and all kinds of places."

Gamadge thought that over. "I don't think it seems so likely that he'd head for home and then pass it like that. Was he coming through the park? There are lots of exits along that way, below and above the Museum."

"No, he didn't come through the park," said Durfee irritably. "He had a regular beat every night. He'd start out just before or soon after dinner, depending on how he felt about it, and first of all he usually rode down, way down to a place in the Village where he used to know a lot of people—writers and theatre people. But the place had changed, and anyway his old friends didn't much care about him any more. He was always talking loud, laying down the law and slamming into the theatres because they wouldn't put on his plays. The writers down there seemed to be able to lay off the drink long enough to get things written or produced, and he annoyed them. I'm talking about after he did get his play done, and it folded."

"Yes, I know."

"That's when he really started this serious drinking. Well, then he'd ride up town a ways and start in on the Third Avenue bars, working up town, you know, from one to the next. Stay a little while in each, always ending up around midnight in a place in the Sixties which is popular and crowded all the time. By midnight he was always full up, ready to wander off. Sometimes he'd wander home. We know that place, it's run by a nice enough man. He remembers seeing Bradlock there that night, but he doesn't remember seeing anybody leave with him. Nobody does. Nobody was paying attention."

"He had no regular friend he'd be likely to wander off with?"

"He had no friends at all, far as we can find out. No use denying it," said Durfee, shaking his head obstinately, "the feller wasn't liked."

"Any special reason, do you know, apart from the ones you mentioned before?" asked Gamadge.

"Well, he'd got to be very run-down in his appearance, of course," said Durfee, thinking it over. "But they wouldn't mind that. I don't quite get it myself. Of course these failures—they turn sour, sometimes. I have the idea he was a snarling type of man, down on everybody. Small-minded. Whisky didn't improve him. Once in a while, as I said, he'd start a fight, and being a little thin feller, he'd get the worst of it. But he didn't get in any fight that last time, he just left this Hanley place and went weaving off.

"His usual plan, from what they tell me, was to walk over to Fifth and take a bus up to the Bradlocks' block, and go home that way. This last night he must have walked up the Avenue, past the block, and cut into the park at that entrance I told you about."

"I suppose he might have done such a thing alone."

"And the thug followed him in. Anyhow, he was found next morning, and he couldn't be identified. Not a thing on him to say who he was. He looked like any tramp by that time, rained on, and in a pair of old corduroy pants he might have brought back from Paris with him. Old coat, home-washed shirt and underwear. He was taken over to the precinct at first, they always are, kept there twenty-four hours, and just before he was sent down to Bellevue, unclaimed, his wife came over and identified him. Nice little woman."

"I've met her. Met the family."

"Well, they had a time. The brother and wife were out of town, and this poor little woman had the worst of it. She read about the hold-up in the papers, and since Bradlock hadn't got home and she couldn't locate him, she called up on the chance and came over. She was a gritty little thing, lots of nerve, but it was tough. She was ashamed about the way he looked, too; had to explain that the brother supported him all right, but like the rest of those soaks, he'd sell anything decent he had if he ran out of cash." Durfee's expression was sardonic. "Too bad I can't give you anything nicer to put in your piece."

"It's all happened before."

"They said he'd been a mighty nice-looking feller too."

"I suppose this must all have been in the papers, Durfee?"

"Every last word of it."

"You said—"

"I said we had a little something more, which didn't get into the papers because it happened after he was out of the news and buried in the family lot, with a nice headstone over him too. I mean we didn't hear about it till afterwards, and I don't think it could interest you or anybody."

"Let's have it, anyway."

"Well, this feller Downey, Brooklyn man, called us up about a week after Bradlock died. He'd been out of town on business—he's some kind of a salesman—and he never saw anything in the papers till he happened on a little write-up in *Time*. He dropped in on us by request and told us the story. Thought we might just possibly be interested. He met Bradlock in an up-town bar the night he was killed, or rather in the early evening. They had something to eat there. Downey said it wasn't seven o'clock. He'd been working here in Manhattan, and wanted a snack before he went home."

"Bradlock hadn't followed his usual routine, then?"

"Not this time, anyway. They had the snack and a few drinks, and Downey said Bradlock was well over the line even then. But he was mighty interesting, and Downey was fascinated. Being a new acquaintance, he got a big kick out of Bradlock's stories and all that talk about his career. He'd never met any such type before.

"Then Downey had to leave, and they walked to Lexington, where Downey could get a subway. Bradlock— you know how these drunks are—hung on to him. Made him walk a ways down Lexington, said he wanted to pay a call. They stopped at an old-fashioned apartment house on a corner, and Bradlock said to wait for him, he wouldn't be a minute, and went on in. Downey wasn't going to wait, but he did, under five minutes; in fact, Downey said it wasn't more than two. Bradlock came back and said his friends weren't home. He rode down to Fourteenth Street with Downey, and got out there.

"Well that wasn't interesting; but just for the fun of it we checked at the apartment; because high or low we couldn't find a soul anywhere that Bradlock seemed to know well at all. These people might have seen him later, and why miss anything?"

"But nobody in the place had ever heard of him."

Gamadge raised his eyebrows.

"He was drunk," explained Durfee. "Just one of the things they do. He might have known somebody there once—Downey said he talked about people long dead as if they were alive, and acted a little crazy anyway. I don't know how he lasted out the evening as well as he did, but they said he got his second wind. Here's the place." Durfee turned a page of the file so that Gamadge could see it. "Quiet, full of respectable people, no reason for them to deny knowing him, especially with all the publicity done with. Anyway, we couldn't connect them up with him, and it was long before he was killed that he stopped there, and he'd seen dozens of people afterwards. So we didn't give it out. Can you use *that* in your piece?"

Gamadge laughed, and got up. "I don't suppose so. Thanks, Durfee. Mighty good of you."

"Not at all. I can see"—Durfee squinted up at him, smiling—"that you couldn't very well get this dope from the family."

"Not very well. No."

"Poor little woman; does she still live there in that annex?"

"Still lives there."

"Avery Bradlock has a lot to be grateful to her for. She took the brunt of it. By the time he got back from the country, his brother was in a nice undertaking parlour, without even a tag on him. Well, be seeing you."

"I hope so."

They shook hands, and Gamadge left the building and took the subway up town. He got out at Forty-second Street, and walked the few blocks across and north to his other club—where he might as easily meet Avery Bradlock as in the little one behind his house, but which Mrs. Bradlock had taken too much for granted to specify. He was early, but he had not wished to keep his luncheon guest waiting.

That guest soon came trotting into the cool and dim vastness of the lobby—a little old gentleman complete with silver-headed walking stick; slim, spritely, and stored with experience. Gamadge introduced himself with deference.

"It's most good of you, Mr. Meriden. I hardly dared suggest it."

"Well, after all," said Mr. Meriden, shaking hands, "apart from the pleasure of meeting you—you're not going to do a book for us, are you? No, I thought not—it was only a step, and I had to lunch somewhere."

"I'm glad you'd at least heard of me, sir." Gamadge piloted Mr. Meriden into the dining-room, and got him to a table in a window.

"You're joking," said Mr. Meriden kindly, "I read all your—no cocktail, no, a glass of sherry if . . ."

The lunch was ordered. When the sherry came, Gamadge ventured to embark on his quest. Mr. Meriden cut it short:

"Perfect shame, but I can't help you at all. The poor lady has dropped out, nobody knows what's become of her. You're doing some work on the nineteen-twenties in Paris—the expatriate writers? Well, poor Isabel Wakes was a promising girl, made a very good job of that book we did—*Some Writing Ladies of France*. We commissioned it, you know."

"Did you, sir?"

"Yes, we saw some of her work in literary reviews. And we knew little Jeremy." Mr. Meriden laughed and shook his head. "Poor little Jeremy, his stuff was much less interesting, very dusty. But it had a certain appeal, it carried on the *Curiosities of Literature* tradition. Luckily he didn't write for money, just to amuse himself. I heard that he was one of the casualties of nineteen hundred and twenty-nine. Quite likely. He died over there, and Isabel came home. So much I know."

"But you think she's still alive, Mr. Meriden?"

Mr. Meriden ate a clam or two before answering. Then he said: "The gossip was that she was doing popular stuff under a pen name. For the pulps, you know. But I have no first-hand information. As a matter of fact, I can quite well imagine her doing that, if she had to make a living. She had tremendous energy, and a strong, effective style, and I should say she was not an idealist."

"Wasn't she?"

"Oh no, a trenchant humour; directed against what we used to call uplift. But I'm very sorry she couldn't turn her hand at something a trifle less . . ." Mr. Meriden looked about him vaguely. "Ephemeral," he finished, and ate another clam.

"How did you hear that she was writing for the pulps under another name, Mr. Meriden?"

"Her agent called up our office, checking on old royalties for her. There were none, of course. He didn't talk to me, didn't even give his name. Took our word for it." Meriden glanced up at Gamadge. "Does that seem at all credible to you, Mr. Gamadge?"

"Entirely credible, Mr. Meriden. I dare say he didn't expect any other news, anyway."

"No. And he didn't give us news of her, or say what her pseudonym was. It was a long time ago. Almost seven years, they tell me at the office. Poor lady, I really wonder what's become of her."

"At least we know what became of Paul Bradlock."

"Paul Bradlock?" Mr. Meriden looked up alertly. "Going to write him up too? That's different."

"Well, he was one of the expatriates, wasn't he?"

"Not when we knew him."

There was a pause while the plates were taken away and the Egg Mornay—Mr. Meriden's choice—came on. At last, when he was well into his spinach, he returned to Paul Bradlock:

"We only did a play of his, you know. Very interesting. He probably came to us through having known Mr. and Mrs. Wakes in Paris. Then, of course, after his tragic death, his wife approached us about the biography."

"I've seen it."

"You know," said Mr. Meriden, suddenly rather serious, "we felt rather as the family did. Get this thing out,

and scotch a lot of irresponsible half-baked stuff, all
personalities and scandal. He was scandalous, of course he
was, but there was more to him than that. We were
disappointed in the result, but the Bradlocks had a good list
for us, and really Mr. Avery Bradlock wasn't much out of
pocket. Very nice man, that."

"I thought so."

"Oh, you've met him? Excellent sort. Upon my word,
I don't know how these things happen in families."

"Paul Bradlock didn't strike you as a good sort, apart
from his unfortunate drinking habits?"

Mr. Meriden, busy with his salad, did not reply for
some moments. At last he said: "This is not for publication."

"Certainly not, if you say so."

Meriden sat back and looked at Gamadge, fixedly and
from under knitted brows. "I never saw a man so disliked. I
didn't like him, none of the editors liked him, the very
switchboard young lady, a pleasant girl, had a kind of—you
might almost say a horror of him."

"Really. I wonder why."

"He was truculent and embittered by that time, and
his hand was against everybody; we can discount all that.
He'd had a disappointing life, and he was financially
dependent. But—I can only say that he radiated ill will. His
play does, you know."

"It does, indeed."

"There's no pathos in the fate of those people, and the
thing never touches tragedy. Empty. Quite empty. But he
could write."

"It's surprising that his wife didn't make her book more
interesting. She seems such a clever woman."

"Oh, very, and a most appealing little thing. Quite
crushed by the tragedy. You know she comes from the
West, and she went to Paris very young to work in a friend's
bookshop. Pretty little creature then, they tell me, quite
ethereal. Just the wife for a young poet."

"I was surprised that she didn't use more letters in the
*Life*."

"On thinking it over, I wasn't. He didn't write letters
himself if he could help it—we could hardly get one out of

him. And when he did"—there was a glint in Mr. Meriden's
eye—"he had an acid pen. He couldn't, simply could not
write an agreeable letter. I should not think that he'd show
up well at either end of any correspondence. He actually
drove the other party into being disagreeable. Question of
temperament, quite apart from alcohol, I should say. I only
hope he reserved some kind of softness for his wife."

"She speaks as if he did."

"Yes, very loyal."

Through the rest of the lunch Mr. Meriden asked
questions instead of answering them, and he asked many.
They all had to do with Gamadge's professional work, and
Gamadge answered them to the best of his ability. Mr.
Meriden seemed to enjoy himself. They parted on the steps
of the club in high good humour with each other.

Gamadge walked down Fifth Avenue to the public
library. His step was slow, his head sunk between his
shoulders, the stoop in his shoulder pronounced. In fact he
had all the air of a baffled man.

# 9

# A Ghost

In the catalogue department Gamadge could find
nowhere in any compilation of or guide to periodical
literature the name of Isabel Wakes. These reference books
did not list the pulps; Gamadge had hoped that Mrs. Wakes
contributed elsewhere under her own name. He moved to
the card indexes, wrote out slips, and then went and sat in
front of the desk in the reading room, waiting for his
number to come up.

He got his books, sat down at a table, and attacked
them. Jeremy Wakes had written three books, not much
more than a collection of anecdotes strung on comment that
was thin and coy:

*Browsings on the Quai*
*Oddities in Old Libraries*
*A Bookman's Diary*

Jeremy Wakes had browsed, but in pastures far from new. The oddities in his works were not as odd now as they had seemed when first noted by people of the past, and the literary discoveries he set forth had not been made by him. He had rehashed old material, frankly confessing it old, and relying on his own chatty style to make it seem as good as new. He was feebly humorous, stuffy in his tastes and queerly conceited.

According to notes on the end pages, some of these pieces had actually appeared in magazines. Gamadge had to remember that Jeremy Wakes was a member of a very old New York family, and that he probably had all sorts of connections with all sorts of important people.

His wife's book was a very different thing. She had had ability, she was rather cruelly amusing—her *Madame de Genlis* was quite delightful in a scathing way—and she had a hard, tough, masculine approach. What on earth had happened to Mrs. Wakes?

He returned the books, and went out into the stream of Fifth Avenue. Disgusted, he got on a bus and rode up to the Eighties. He walked across to Lexington, and stood in front of the old brick five-story apartment where Paul Bradlock had called—and stayed "less than five minutes, in fact no more than two," on the last evening of his life.

It was a big place, with stores in the basement. It had no canopy and no doorman, and when Gamadge entered the dark, spacious lobby, he felt as if it had no inhabitants. It was as quiet as death. Old panelling rose head-high; a stairway curved from landing to landing, the skylight was a pale smear among shadows. No elevator, and so far as Gamadge could see, no list of tenants anywhere.

He turned back to the vestibule, where a disheartening message scribbled on a card informed him that the superintendent was on the premises from eight to ten in the mornings and from four to six in the afternoons. It was now only half-past three.

The card was wedged above a little knob in the panelling. Gamadge shoved this aside; it disclosed a typed list of names, which he read with no recognition and with dwindling interest. But he doggedly went through it again, and this time stopped midway, hunched forward, and gazed intently at one item:

Imogen Weekes. 52B.

Could Isabel Wakes be using an alias as well as a pen name, and was that the reason why she had dropped out of sight? People often did stick to their initials, probably because they had marked belongings and wanted to go on using them.

Bradlock had called here on the last night of his life. As a very old friend, he would be likely to know Mrs. Wakes's new name; but it had conveyed nothing to the police, nor would the name of Wakes have conveyed anything. She would have been pretty safe in denying the acquaintance-ship.

Feeling every little doubt in his own mind, Gamadge began to climb. On the third floor, in the rear, twin doors confronted him. One was marked 52A, the other 52B. Looking around him, he saw two similar doors in each wall, but only one of each pair was numbered; it looked as though the rear apartment had been cut into two.

He rang at 52B. After a short pause the door was opened, and a tall figure stood facing him against the light. A woman built on big lines, but with not much flesh on her bones now; a woman gone to seed. A great mass of greying hair was drawn back from her broad forehead and coiled untidily; grey eyes, set flat in a pale face, looked at Gamadge without curiosity. She wore a long silk robe that had once been an evening coat; its brocade was tarnished, its fur collar matted down like old plush. There were frayed satin sandals on her feet.

Gamadge said: "I do hope I'm not disturbing you, Mrs. Wakes."

Whatever Mrs. Wakes had lost, she had retained—or

perhaps acquired—the gift of silence. She stood with her hand on the knob, perfectly quiet, showing no interest.

"My name is Gamadge," he went on, "Henry Gamadge. I do a little writing. I've just had lunch with Mr. Meriden, the publisher—"

She interrupted in a hoarse, rather rough voice: "I didn't think the old boy knew where I was. Did Malone give me away? I told him not to. Skin him for it—not that it matters. What can I do for you?"

"I'm interested in literary byways. Of course I've read your book—French women writers."

"Oh, that. Thought it was dead long ago. I only did that for the money, on commission; I read up for it. Don't know a thing that isn't in the book itself. I couldn't even give you the sources now. Can't be a bit of help to you."

"It's the authors I'm interested in, Mrs. Wakes. Your husband's work, yours, all the research work done at that time abroad."

She paused before saying anything more. Then she dropped her hand from the knob. "Poor old Jeremy, his books were no good; but he got a lot of amusement doing them. You might as well come in."

The door opened directly on a large, high, ugly room, too narrow for its depth and with its one tall window asymmetrically placed to the extreme left in the rear wall. A big desk-table stood in front of it, heavily laden with the equipment of a working writer—papers, blank or typewritten, crushed carbon sheets, were heaped and strewn over the whole top of the desk, and some of them were on the floor. The typewriter emerged from a mass of them. Erasers, worn down to their metal hubs, pencils and pens, clips and a little oil-can, were strewn over an open, dog's-eared dictionary and some other books. Gamadge looked at this mess with sympathy.

"I'm afraid I am disturbing you horribly," he said.

"Doesn't matter. Sit down. I always quit work at four, anyway."

Mrs. Wakes herself sat down in the desk-chair, and Gamadge took a sagging wicker one opposite her. He glanced about him. There was a studio couch in the corner between the west and north wall, and at its foot an open doorway led into darkness. There was a dressing table behind a screen, another table, a chair or two, a ragged Persian rug, cut down to size. The window curtains, of faded madras, were shoved back to give what little western light came from over the house-tops.

Mrs. Wakes followed his glance. "They cut some of these apartments in half to give themselves more rents. I used to have the whole rear, but it was too big for me. Too much bother to take care of. Have to be independent of cleaning women these days."

Gamadge thought the place looked as if Mrs. Wakes still found it too much bother to take care of. He said: "Nice old places—the ceilings are so high."

"Yes. Nice big bathrooms too, lots of space for cooking. And the iceman doesn't have to be repaired."

"You're right about that." Mrs. Wakes had a tonic cynicism that rather pleased him. He said: "I do hope you won't think it impertinent of me if I say that I wish you hadn't stopped signing your own stuff, Mrs. Wakes."

She laughed. "Know what my own stuff is?"

"Well, no, but your Meriden book—"

"You think my Meriden book would pay the rent?" She shoved a book on the desk towards Gamadge, still laughing. "Don't give the poor girl away—I mean Gillian."

Gamadge picked up the book, which had a lively jacket, and read the title: *And Now I Am an Extra. By Gillian Giles*.

"Went big in serial," Mrs. Wakes told him, "so they made a book of it. Doesn't often happen. I don't do big names."

Gamadge said respectfully: "I'd get the tragedy of the title better if I knew who Gillian was—or had been."

"Oh, she was quite a well-known silent movie star. But now"—and she laughed again—"she needs money as much as I do."

"She's lucky in her ghost."

"Oh, they don't want me to *write*," said Mrs. Wakes carelessly. "That would spoil everything. They just want the formula. We cater to a simple public. You won't give me away, will you?"

"Shouldn't think of it. You're very sporting."

"One must live, in spite of what that fellow said. *I* see the necessity. And the other fellow was right—when he said that nobody but a fool writes except for money."

"Doctor Johnson never meant it like that," protested Gamadge earnestly. "He never meant it at all. Catch him compromising or writing down to a public! Excuse me; but I hate people to quote that—and quote it wrong, too."

Mrs. Wakes did not take offence. She said tolerantly: "I used to feel that way myself, but *I* had money then."

"You have something there."

"Well, let's see, what can I do for you? You must be hard up for a subject if you want to write about Jeremy's books."

"I'm particularly interested in him, to be quite frank, as a friend of Paul Bradlock's."

Mrs. Wakes's elbow slid sideways over the papers on the desk-top. After a moment she said roughly: "Jeremy knew him as others did. I haven't anything suitable for memoirs."

"Haven't you? I was wondering if he didn't sponge on you too—during his later years here in New York. That night he was killed, for instance, when he stopped in to see you."

Mrs. Wakes had ceased to move. She sat, her head a little lifted, looking past Gamadge with slate-grey eyes.

"The police know he came, of course," said Gamadge in a casual tone. "But it was early in the evening, and there was no reason why any friend of his here should be involved. And it's quite understandable that you should have denied knowing him afterwards. All that unpleasant publicity."

Mrs. Wakes might not have heard him. After a bleak moment she said without moving: "Don't I hear a tap dripping?"

Gamadge heard nothing. He did not speak as she got slowly out of her chair and walked across the room to the doorway opposite. She went through it; Gamadge turned in his chair to watch her.

He could see that the door led only to a small lobby, with no exit to the hall. She turned left and disappeared. He relaxed, and sat facing the desk.

Presently she returned, and before she passed him he was conscious of a strong smell of brandy. She stood for a moment with her back to him, one hand on the desk. Then she turned, sat down, and fumbled in the litter on the desk for a package of cigarettes. Gamadge lighted hers, and one for himself.

Leaning back, she asked: "Why interview me about Paul Bradlock? I hardly knew him. If he came here that evening he probably wanted to borrow a book. He'd know I had a lot of Jeremy's old books. He'd certainly know I hadn't money for him or anybody. Why don't you interview his wife?"

"She presumably said her say in her book."

Mrs. Wakes laughed, a little drowsily. "I didn't ghost that!"

"You'd have made something better of it."

"I never see the woman." She leaned back and turned her head a little away, pale wisps of her hair straying against the faded cushion. "We never bothered with that girl; just somebody Paul picked up in the bookshop. No talent, but she'd be quite shocked at what I do now. So would Paul. Always very highbrow."

Her voice was blurred. Gamadge wondered how many drinks she had had before he arrived; certainly there had been no evidence of them.

"Must eat, whatever they say."

Her sentence trailed off. Gamadge rose; the interview was over. He left her to all appearances half asleep; his watch said four o'clock.

The dark landings were still deserted. Gamadge went down the stairs slowly, and blinked when he got out into the sunlight. He took a bus home. Clara greeted him in the library:

"Tea's ready, and your friend Mr. Iverson has been calling you ever since one. He's left a message for you."

"No! Has he?" Gamadge was diverted. "Where is it?"

"Beside the telephone in the hall."

Gamadge went and found it. It was in Clara's hand: *Will Mr. Gamadge very kindly call on Mrs. Paul Bradlock any time after four o'clock? Very urgent, he will understand that a conference is in order. If no telephone message received, we'll expect him. Iverson.*

"Are you going?" asked Clara.

"Am I going? Of course."

"I thought you said they didn't want you to look at those letters."

"They just want to talk about them."

"Why on earth should you rush up there for that? It seems to me that these people have a good deal of nerve," said Clara.

"I'd like to know how much they *have* got." Gamadge, still amused, sat down on the chesterfield. "Anyhow, there's plenty of time for tea."

"I should hope so."

Half an hour later he took a cab up to the iron gates, paid it off, and stood for a minute looking down the side yard, past the big Mexican urns, to the corner of the studio door that was visible from the street. How remote the squat, ugly little house looked, hidden away and hemmed in by taller buildings, cut off from direct sunlight at any hour; cut off from the Bradlock house by no more than a few yards of passage, but in spirit how immeasurably far! Two locked doors between; the sneak-thief excuse was good enough, but Gamadge thought the Bradlock side had been locked against more imminent invasions than that.

It had been locked against Paul Bradlock, and the habit persisted still. Avery Bradlock had no confidence in his sister-in-law's friends, left-overs from wilder days.

As for Vera Bradlock, she locked her doors and went her own way. Gamadge walked down the alley, climbed her steps, and rang.

# 10

# The Book of the Lion

The little pink-nosed girl opened the door. This time she was all ready to leave, one arm in her shiny grey coat, a magenta beret crushed down on her head; she looked as if she meant to leap past him and away.

Gamadge, on the step, addressed her pleasantly: "Well, Miss Sally; why do you plunge out of the house every time I come into it?"

"I have to go."

"Why not stay this time and see the fun? And where's your gentleman friend?"

"I don't know. I suppose he's asleep." She looked up at Gamadge, and vaguely from side to side. Then with a glance over her shoulder, she said again: "I have to go."

"It's just like sitting through a movie twice," complained Gamadge. "Same action every time. And you fade out."

She gave him a nervous look, ducked past him, and ran down the steps. Gamadge watched her for a moment as she hurried along the path to the gates, her handbag clutched to her side, her topcoat still hanging from one shoulder. Then he went into the studio and closed the door behind him.

The studio was very dark at this hour of the day, uncertain light filtering in from the two narrow windows that overlooked the side wall of the neighbouring apartment house, across the deep well of the service alley between. Gamadge saw Iverson advancing to meet him, but for a moment he did not make out the effaced figure of Mrs. Paul Bradlock. She was sitting in front of the fireplace to the extreme right of the door, beyond the entrance to the connecting passage.

Iverson looked amused, embarrassed, and apologetic. He said: "Mr. Gamadge, we appreciate this fully; but we counted on you. We really knew you'd respond to our plaintive cry."

"Least I could do, don't you think?" Gamadge smiled.

"You were very naughty," said Mrs. Bradlock, and there was no embarrassment on her impudent little face. "Curiosity killed the cat, I understand."

"Now, Vera, now Vera!" Iverson, laughing, went across to the piano, where a tray had been set out with whisky, a siphon, ice and tumblers. "We're in no position to make countercharges. Unconditional surrender. Have a drink, Gamadge, before we embark on this highly confidential confession?"

"I really don't think—I've just had tea."

"Tea! That won't support you."

"The drink of heroes." Gamadge went over and sat down on the couch beside Mrs. Bradlock. There was a low fire in the grate now, and he was glad of it; the chill of the place was awful.

"Well," said Iverson, bringing a glass to Mrs. Bradlock and then going back to fill his own, "I need more assistance than tea would give me—if I ever drank it." He added: "And so does Vera, but I want you to keep in mind the fact that she was always strictly within her rights."

"I realize that."

Mrs. Bradlock sipped her whisky in silence, that little smile lingering on her face. It was in her eyes, too, as she watched Gamadge demurely. Iverson came and sat down on Gamadge's right. He pulled a standard ashtray towards the group, and they all lighted cigarettes.

"Now then," he said. "Shall I take off, Vera, and will you supply notes?"

"Please, Hill."

"Well, Gamadge." Iverson crossed his knees, and put his tumbler down on a coffee table. "Let me begin by admitting—what you already knew, or you wouldn't have sent that delightful young Mr. Malcolm to call on me—that Vera and I practised an innocent deception on Avery Bradlock."

"But such an elaborate mystification," said Gamadge. "That's my only excuse for my behaviour. The puzzle tempted me beyond my strength."

"It would! But we don't quite know how you came to guess that there was a puzzle." He looked at Gamadge, very alert, and Mrs. Bradlock's face also showed interest.

"Merely the timeliness of your arrival with your cheque," answered Gamadge, laughing. "I thought it looked as if Mrs. Bradlock wanted to avoid showing her papers at all costs. Could she have disposed of them before? I really had to know. Mr. Malcolm, by the way, is very discreet."

"I hope so!" Iverson joined in the laughter, and so did Mrs. Paul Bradlock.

She said: "We never would have dared do it if we'd known you were coming that night."

"Didn't Mrs. Avery tell you?" asked Gamadge.

"She only said that Avery had consulted an expert, and that a friend had told him people sold letters for large sums. It was after he came home that he exploded his bomb—about you; and I'd already told him that Hill Iverson was going to buy the papers."

"I hope Mr. Iverson will get his money back?"

Iverson looked at Mrs. Bradlock. "How about it, Vera? What's Avery going to do with that cheque?" He was grinning.

"We'll have to wait, Hill." She gave him a plaintive look. "Can you trust me?"

"I'll have to. At least we know Avery won't embezzle it."

"I thought it would make such a good impression if I just handed it over."

"It did; didn't it, Gamadge?"

"On Avery Bradlock, it most certainly did."

"Oh Lord, Vera, if we'd known then that Gamadge was a practising criminologist! Suspecting poor widows and their charitable friends!"

"What would you have done," asked Gamadge, "if you *had* known I was coming?"

"Hanged if I know. Got the box out earlier, I suppose,

before you arrived. You wouldn't have bothered with a *fait accompli*, I hope?"

"We mustn't blame Mr. Gamadge for our predicament, though," said Vera, leaning forward to drop her ash in the tray. "It goes back farther than that. It goes back to that awful man who put the whole idea into Avery's head at lunch—that busybody Williamson, or whatever his name is. What a nuisance. After that I had to produce letters, or at least convince Avery that there were letters. The trouble was that I'd said there were." She looked up at Gamadge, and for the first time since he had met her he saw what he thought was sincerity in her eyes. Sincerity and cold anger. "So that I'd have an excuse for staying on and writing the book. I said I wouldn't let anybody else use Paul's letters." She sat up, shrugged, drank some whisky. "I needn't have mentioned them at all, I suppose. There were almost none—Paul didn't keep letters, or anything else. I used what I had. Unfortunately, Avery has a great regard for the truth."

Iverson said: "You wouldn't understand, Gamadge, unless you knew Avery Bradlock, but you probably know his type. A fair man, an honest man, but he has a strong feeling that he's done a lot for his brother's wife. Being a business man first, last and always, he kept accounts, he watched every penny, he felt that he must be consulted at every turn. The Paul Bradlock estate is in debt to him for God knows how much—the biography, everything, Vera had nothing. Can you see her telling Bradlock last night that she'd been selling unlisted assets and pocketing money?"

"But she didn't," objected Gamadge.

Iverson looked at Vera and laughed. "I'm getting a little ahead of myself. Can you see her even telling Bradlock that she'd falsely declared non-existent assets? No. He'd be very touchy about that. And as for his doing so much for her—well, let's be frank in all things at last. I was fond of Paul Bradlock, Gamadge, I knew him in drama circles in his playwriting days. But when I got to know him at home and met his wife—let me tell you what she's done for the Bradlocks, and then perhaps you'll see where my loyalty shifted to."

"No, Hill," said Vera. "Don't."

"Sorry, Vera, we'd better be frank with our criminologist. For fifteen years she had the whole care and responsibility, Gamadge, in the matter of Paul Bradlock: a hopeless, evil-tempered drunkard. Do you know at all what that means? She was the one who sat up at night, searched the dives, paid the fines, stood between the house next door and publicity. Half the time nobody realized that there was any connection between Paul Bradlock and his respectable brother. Avery paid their living expenses and gave them a roof; who's in debt now to whom?"

"I told Mrs. Paul Bradlock last night," said Gamadge, "before I knew any details, that I didn't think she owed her brother-in-law anything."

"No. But"—Iverson leaned forward, pointing at Gamadge with his cigarette—"suppose she *had* secretly sold unlisted assets? And put the proceeds into an annuity? And was only waiting for a good business opportunity, and an improvement in the housing situation, to leave this place forever?"

Gamadge said after a moment: "I don't suppose in that case that Bradlock would expect reimbursement."

"But how about the Bradlocks' goodwill? People like the Avery Bradlocks can make it very unpleasant for people like Vera Bradlock, who has no background, no friends in this part of the world—thanks to Paul—and no business references *except* Avery. Her side of it could be made to look black—I'm not denying it. Legally she's all right; otherwise . . ." He shook his head. "I've been trying to show you both sides. People will say she was evading her just debts. I say—I said so to her at the time—that she had no debts where the Bradlocks were concerned. The money she realized wasn't more than enough to keep her comfortably."

"At her age," agreed Gamadge, "annuity rates wouldn't be high. But—excuse me—I think it might have been safe to tell Avery Bradlock all about it in the first place. Why not?"

"Ah, now we're coming to it." Iverson sat back and smiled. "She couldn't."

"Couldn't?" Gamadge looked mildly inquiring.

"Couldn't."

Vera said: "Tell him, Hill."

Iverson, his gaze fixed on Gamadge's face, put his hand into an inner breast pocket and brought it out holding a folded paper. "You'd better hold on to your chair, Gamadge."

"I'm prepared for anything."

"Not for this." The other, his eyes still holding Gamadge's, asked: "Did you ever hear of *The Book of the Lion*?"

Gamadge, his cigarette half-way to his mouth, asked after a pause: "The what?"

"I see you have," said Vera in her small voice.

"I've heard of a *Book of the Lion*," said Gamadge, staring at her, "yes."

"So far as I know," said Iverson, chuckling, "there has only been one."

"Are you referring by any chance," asked Gamadge, "to one of the lost books of Chaucer?"

"I am."

"What about it?"

Iverson turned his head to look at Vera Bradlock. He said: "You know, Vera, I think we've really got him going. Why don't you take it up here? Then I'll cut in with the technicalities."

She threw her cigarette into the fire; a long, accurate arc. "Paul had no safe-deposit box, Mr. Gamadge, naturally; he had nothing of value to put in one, so far as he knew. Please remember that; it's important to remember that for Paul's sake."

Gamadge nodded.

"But he had one of those flat tin cashboxes," she went on, "an old-fashioned thing that he had in Paris from the time I first knew him. You know in France people liked to keep masses of paper money lying around—in desk drawers, bureaus, everywhere. Paul kept his franc notes in this box.

"When there were no more franc notes, he kept odds and ends in it—receipts, scraps of manuscript, antique coins of small value, papers relating to literary controversy, newspaper clippings. After he was dead, when I was looking for material for my book, I hunted up that box. It was in the attic."

Gamadge looked behind him and up to the trap in the ceiling.

"Much easier than you'd think," said Vera, following his thought. "The trap-door works mechanically—what do you call it? Counterweight or something? You just push and it stays up as far as you like. I got the box, and the key was lost. I had to pry it open. I found all the old stuff, or I suppose it was the stuff I remembered, but I also found a dog's-eared torn old roll of manuscript. Even I could see that it was old, partly on vellum, too; but it had no title. I thought it was something Paul had picked up in one of the rummage sales he was always going to in the back streets in Paris. Once he found quite a good portfolio of old drawings and sold them."

She took another cigarette out of the box on the coffee table, and Gamadge leaned forward to light it for her. She smoked for a few moments in silence. Then she went on:

"I showed it to Hill Iverson. He found the last page, and the author's name, in the middle of the roll. He sorted the pages out, and after we'd more or less realized what it was, or seemed to be—we had to do a little research in the libraries—Hill took the thing to a collector who happened to be here in New York; a well-known collector, an expert in such things. He"—she glanced at the paper in Iverson's fingers—"typed a description."

"And here," said Iverson, handing Gamadge the folded sheet, "here it is, or rather a copy of it."

Gamadge unfolded the paper. He sat back to catch the last of the daylight, and read as follows:

Paper and vellum manuscript, measuring eight and one half by five and one half inches.
Two quires. In each quire, leaves 1, 6, 7, and 12 are of vellum, the rest paper. Ruled margins enclose a space five and one half by three and one quarter inches. The manuscript is neatly written

in one hand of the middle of the fifteenth century.
There is no title, but at the end of the last page,
which was the end of the work, on folio 72 *recto*,
is found the following colophon (corner lost):

> *Heere is endid the boke of the Leoun by*
> *Geffrey Chaucier of whose soule Jhesu*
> *Crist have mer*

The work itself, a dream-vision allegory in
octosyllabic couplets, meets all the established
linguistic tests as a genuine poem by Chaucer, and
there is no doubt that it is the hitherto lost work,
entitled THE BOOK OF THE LION, named by Chaucer himself in the list of his writings in the
"Retraction" at the end of the *Canterbury Tales*.

Gamadge finished reading. He sat looking at the paper,
silent, while Iverson and Mrs. Bradlock looked at him.
They were very still.

At last Gamadge looked up at Iverson. He pointed to
the typed page. "Your expert wrote that?"

"He let me copy it. That's my copy."

"It's an excellent piece of work. *It* meets all the
requirements"—Gamadge smiled—"too."

"Oh, our man was a scholar."

"Evidently." Gamadge knitted his brows. "*Was?*"

"I'm coming to that. He explained that of course there
are no Chaucer manuscripts in existence—nothing in
Chaucer's own hand, you know; poor Vera and I had to be
told so! He was quite shocked at our ignorance. He
explained, as I say, that this beast fable (a fashion of the
times) had been copied from the original by a fifteenth-
century scribe. And he said that this Lion thing had been so
utterly lost that nobody even knew there had ever been a
copy made."

"That's so."

"Our man was knocked flat by the manuscript—by the
whole thing."

"Naturally. I feel limp myself, and I'm no Chaucerian."

"To him it was almost like a miracle. He checked up, as you see from his description, but very discreetly, and we—er—sold it to him."

"I hope," said Gamadge in a faint voice, "that you got your price?"

"Oh, we had to let him fix it; but we could depend on him. One hundred thousand dollars. He said that would be an approximately fair market price. What do you say, Gamadge?"

"At a guess, that would be about it."

"He stipulated absolute secrecy until he decided just what to do; of course he meant to keep it, but he wanted to build it up for the world. Handle the publicity right. We left it all to him—when I tell you who it was, you'll see why. I could help Vera there. I knew you could trust Eigenstern."

*"Eigenstern!"*

"Yes," said Iverson gently, "that's the catch. Eigenstern. That's why you've heard nothing about this great literary discovery, Gamadge, and never will hear anything. Eigenstern took *The Book of the Lion* back with him by plane to California, where he lived; took it back as a top secret. You know what happened."

"I know what happened." Gamadge relaxed for the first time. He leaned back, smoking and looking at the fire.

"The plane went down. Eigenstern, and *The Book of the Lion*, and every other person and thing on board, were burned up in that mountain ravine. The *Lion* is lost again—forever."

"How lucky that Mrs. Bradlock got her money."

"Wasn't it? Eigenstern—for greater secrecy—paid it over in hard cash. Or shall we say"—he laughed—"folding money?"

"You didn't take a copy of the manuscript?"

"My dear man, do you think Eigenstern would have allowed that? Oh, I know what a tragedy it is, and must seem to a man like you. It did to me. But Vera had her money, and we've had nearly two years to get over the shock. You can see, I suppose, why we can't even tell the story?"

Gamadge said after a pause: "No proof except this typed page."

"Would you call it proof, if somebody came to you with it and with nothing more?"

"No. It's no good as evidence that *The Book of the Lion* ever was discovered."

"But you do see"—Mrs. Bradlock spoke in a low voice—"why we couldn't talk about it, apart from lack of evidence?"

"To Avery Bradlock, you mean?" He glanced at her.

"To anybody!"

"Didn't Eigenstern ask where it had come from?"

Iverson sighed heavily. "What could we tell him? What did we know? And how could we object if Eigenstern swore us to secrecy while he checked up? He took his time about it, I can tell you. Vera didn't get a penny until he'd pretty well satisfied himself that no such treasure had been lost out of any collection abroad. Nice if he'd paid a hundred thousand, and then some old spider in France or England had laid claim to it! But we could tell him that Paul haunted the sales and the old back rooms of shops. You remember that the last page was hidden in those acres of fifteenth-century manuscript; and thank God I *didn't* have to copy them!"

"What was Eigenstern going to say about that?"

"About where the manuscript came from?"

"Well, yes; the Chaucerians would have liked to know."

Vera said suddenly and angrily: "Anybody could see that Paul never knew what it was! Wouldn't *he* have sold it if he'd known?"

"Er—not if he couldn't account satisfactorily . . ."

Vera stirred in her corner. "We've told you!"

"But he did keep it, you know; in his tin box."

Iverson said amicably: "Face it, Vera; it's only what Eigenstern said. It's what anybody would say. Face it. We knew Paul. Whatever his faults, he wasn't a thief. Say he was in exactly our position; couldn't be sure it wasn't stolen property, couldn't bring it out into the open without giving someone away. One thing we do know, he was damned

loyal. Here's what Eigenstern proposed, Gamadge: the
thing was genuine on its merits. He'd exhibit it on its
merits, and say it had been bought by a dead friend among
old papers—perfectly credible, just, what happened, so far
as we know. Then if he were pressed too hard he *would* give
them Paul's name, and tell them the circumstances of the
discovery; but by that time Vera would have been out of
this rathole and far away, where she wouldn't have to see
Avery at all. It's his feelings she's thinking of."

Gamadge handed Iverson the description of the lost
*Lion*. He said pleasantly: "And now we have only one more
question to dispose of, haven't we?"

"A dozen if you like." Iverson laughed and drained his
highball. "But I think we've covered it."

"I only want to know why you told the story to *me*."

"My dear man, you ask us that?"

"I ask you that. You and Mrs. Bradlock explained the
comedy of the non-existent papers; why explain the tragedy
of the *Lion*, which was entirely beside the question of the
papers? I knew nothing about it at all."

Vera said with gentle sarcasm: "But you'd wanted to
know so much!"

"We've had a taste of your quality," agreed Iverson.
"Suppose you took it into your head later on to inquire into
the source of poor Vera's income? We don't know what
facilities you have in those directions. How much better for
us to tell you ourselves; now you may not feel that you have
to discuss the matter with Avery Bradlock."

"That's why we told you the rest of it," said Vera.
"Somehow, I thought you might be willing to keep the
whole thing from Avery—the papers, and the *Lion*, and
everything—since there were no papers, and the *Lion* is
lost."

"You were right, Mrs. Bradlock," Gamadge rose. "I
shouldn't dream of repeating your story about the papers,
or about *The Book of the Lion*, to your brother-in-law."

"It's rather a tempting story," she said wistfully.

"Count on me, I'll never tell that story to Avery Bradlock."

Iverson, on his feet and facing Gamadge, said comfortably: "I did rather think that your interest was academic."

"Oh, it was. I'm afraid it shows me up in a poor light, too."

"Perfectly right to take all knowledge for your province." Iverson addressed Mrs. Bradlock without turning to look at her: "Shall we forgive him, Vera?"

"Yes, of course."

Gamadge smiled down at her. "I ought to thank you for that tantalizing glimpse—the description."

"We thought you'd probably enjoy it."

"It's proof that you got the opinion of an expert. It would stand up under the most pedantic scrutiny."

Iverson showed him to the door. "Tell Mr. Malcolm," he said, looking arch, "that if he does me the honour of calling again, I'll be more hospitable next time. Charming fellow. Did you really find out who murdered his stepmother?"

"I did, I'm sorry to say."

"Glad you have compunctions."

Iverson closed the door after him. Gamadge walked down the path, past the blank wall across the alley on his right, past the Bradlocks' bow window on his left, to the street. It was less than a quarter to six. He did not hail a cab or take a bus, but walked straight over to Lexington Avenue and down. By six o'clock he was climbing the stairs to Mrs. Wakes's apartment.

# 11

# Return

The bell had a loud, harsh strident note like one of those old-fashioned gongs that used to be attached to the very door itself. New wiring for the new room-and-bath apartment. Gamadge rang, waited and rang again.

She must be out, he thought; she couldn't be as fast asleep as all that, not after one shot of neat brandy—for he was more and more convinced, as he remembered the earlier visit, that she had been cold sober when he came. He was pretty sure that sudden drowsiness had been a perfectly unanswerable way of getting rid of him. Or had she gone back to her solitary bottle after he left, and quietly drunk herself into oblivion by six in the afternoon?

That bell ought to wake the dead. He tried it again, as steps sounded on the wooden stairs.

An elderly man, narrow of jaw and thin in the chest, came as far as the landing. He had a couple of tools in his hand—a wrench and a screwdriver. He asked: "Ain't she there?"

"She doesn't seem to be."

"She wanted me to come up before I left, fix a pipe." The man had a sour look, he was probably not well tipped. "Old place is falling to pieces, and the landlord won't do nothing while the rent's froze." He came and stood beside Gamadge, looking at the door. "She was going to be in."

"You're the superintendent?"

"That's who."

"You have short hours for such a big place."

"Catch the owners giving them a resident, with the rents—"

"I know."

"They're glad to be here at these prices, don't let me

75

give you the wrong impression. Nice big rooms. These people"—he glanced about him as if the tenants were cringing under his eye—"they're mostly retired professional people, lots of women. I don't know where they'll go to when the rents go up."

"Perhaps all the apartments will be cut down, like Mrs.—Weekes's."

"Wouldn't be surprised. Well, it's funny, she said she'd be here. I got to go in, I'm overdue home. If it ain't the right pipe—that's up to her."

"I'd like to leave a note myself. Mrs. Weekes doesn't seem to be in the telephone book . . ." Gamadge thought he could venture on that hypothesis. "I don't think she has a telephone. I didn't see one when I was here before."

"No, she hasn't got one."

The superintendent rang twice, loud and long. Then, with a side glance of disgust at his unwilling confidant, he took out his pass key and fitted it into the lock. He put his knee against the door and pushed. "Every lock in the building sticks," he said.

The door swung wide.

"And loose hinges," added the superintendent.

They stood looking into the dim room. Mrs. Wakes had not put her papers away or covered her typewriter. A breeze from the west fluttered an edge of a curtain. The superintendent said: "Well, you can write the note while I—" he started for the lobby, and stopped.

Gamadge had not moved from the doorway; now he went across the room and bent over the figure on the couch.

"Out like a light," said the superintendent. "Early for her, and I'm surprised she started in before I came. They always think nobody knows about it."

Mrs. Wakes looked as though she had barely made the trip to the day bed. She had sat down, leaned back against the pillow, and gone to sleep with her feet on the floor. Gamadge lifted her hand.

"What's the use distoib her?" asked the superintendent irascibly. "Take an expoit to wake her out of that."

Gamadge straightened. "*You* have a telephone down-stairs, haven't you?"

"Listen, what's the use calling a doctor? She don't need one. Didn't you ever see a blot-out before?"

"The police will bring their own doctor."

"Police?" The superintendent's voice rose in a croak. "She's dead."

"What are you . . ." the superintendent moved forward and stared. "I tell you she's . . ."

"Will you go down and ring the precinct? Or do you want to stay here while I do it?"

The superintendent leaned forward, and studied the grey face. Then he stood upright. He said: "For a fact, I'll go."

"Ask for Lieutenant Durfee, will you?"

"Thank God you got a friend there." The superintendent hurried away. Gamadge shut the door, and then went back to look at the leaden profile against the red cushion. His face was blank, his hands hung loosely at his sides. Presently he turned and surveyed the room, frowning. He walked into the little dark lobby, which contained nothing but a wardrobe trunk, and then turned left and went into a big tiled bathroom.

There was an old tub raised on claw feet, a washstand and medicine cabinet, an electric plate and a gas ring on a small zinc-covered table. There was a little tin ice-box, under which water dripped into a pan. A closet door, half open, disclosed part of Mrs. Wakes's wardrobe, and shelves crowded with dishes and containers.

On the ledge of the washbasin lay a half-pint brandy flask, with a little brandy in it; against it had rolled a glass tube, thin as a straw, with white dust and a fragment of white pellet at the bottom of it. It had no label. A tumbler stood back where the ledge was wider; it contained dregs of brandy.

Gamadge went back into the sitting-room, sat in the wicker chair, and looked at Mrs. Wakes. She had had a quiet death, and Gamadge did not think that she would have blamed him too much; she had been a ghost in more ways than one for so long.

The radio men came in a very few minutes, and after them the usual crowd, the usual routine. After the first turmoil was over, Gamadge was able to get down to the superintendent's basement and telephone Clara that he would be very late for dinner; but that was after Durfee had come. An hour later the room was cleared, and he and Durfee sat facing each other across the desk. They were both smoking.

# 12

# Half a Pint

Durfee said: "I always like your rigmaroles. I've heard a lot of 'em, and I've enjoyed 'em." He fluttered the fingers of both hands, then picked up his cigarette again. "This one, no. Not this time."

Gamadge said nothing; his eyes were on a framed photograph of a bridge over the Seine, which hung just above Durfee's head.

"It's the plainest case of suicide I ever saw," continued Durfee, "it can't be anything but suicide, and you supplied the motive yourself." He leaned forward and tapped the desk. "Don't you admit you're responsible for this woman's death?"

"In a way, yes, I am."

"In a way? In a way? What happens? You come here— bust in on her this afternoon and give her the shock of her life; tell her we know Paul Bradlock called here the evening he was killed. And you even let her think we know *who* he called on. And let me tell you, Gamadge, you overstepped there."

Gamadge looked sideways at Durfee, and then back at the picture. Durfee put up both hands, palm outwards, and shoved them towards Gamadge as though he were pushing him off.

"I know, I know, I give you that," he said angrily. "You found out who she was, and you connected her up with Paul Bradlock."

"They were connected before. She was connected with him twenty years ago in Paris."

"She was, and who else? Anyway, I'll give you that. It's pretty plain, from what you say, that she saw him that evening."

"Since he was here such a short time, it almost looks as if she were all ready for him," remarked Gamadge.

"Even if she didn't have a telephone. Wait a minute, did she have one then, two years ago?" Durfee thought. "No, I guess not. Well, he came here to tell her something or to hear something, or to give her something."

"Or to get something," said Gamadge dreamily.

"Which he dragged all over town with him. For all I know," said Durfee, "she followed him up and down to all the saloons, and then took him walking in the park and killed him. With"—Durfee glanced around the room sourly—"with something she had with her, slid down in her umbrella. In spite of the fact that there's no evidence he wasn't murdered by a hold-up man." Durfee looked up at Gamadge from under lowered lids, scowling. "Another motive for her to commit suicide, if she thought you were on to that. Truth is, Gamadge, you have murder on the brain. You came in this morning and asked about Paul Bradlock's death, with no better reason than some funny business about those letters, which Iverson and Mrs. Paul explained to you to-day."

Gamadge lifted his head and gazed at the ceiling as if in prayer. He said: "I've just told you that I wondered whether she hadn't sold something of value, which Paul Bradlock had been murdered for."

This time Durfee put his hands up as before, but motioned with them violently to the left, the gesture of one who tries to disencumber himself of something soft and smothering. He said: "You have murder on the brain. What happens? You come here and explode this bomb under the woman. She gets up and goes into her bathroom and she pours a shot of brandy into a tumbler and empties a tube of quarter-grain morphia tablets into the shot. That's black market morphia, or it would have had the label with the serial number on it; but it's a twenty-tablet tube, five grains. There must have been eight to twelve tablets in there, perhaps more—I bet they find all of three grains in her. I wouldn't be surprised if they got most of the five. Doc says she'd be dead in half an hour, and she *was* dead in half an hour, or just about. When you left, she was dying. Wasn't she?"

"Yes, she was dying."

"The times are right. You left at four. Doc was here by seven. He says she died more than two hours before he got here, and so far as he could tell it might have been near three. Feller, you were lucky I came."

"Well," said Gamadge, looking at him mildly, "I sent for you."

"Yes," replied Durfee, almost at the top of his voice, "and what do you tell me when I get here? That the woman didn't commit suicide, oh no, she was murdered. She was murdered! With morphia in the glass she drank out of, none in the half-pint flask, and the container there with morphia in it, and she comes back here with brandy on her breath and goes right to sleep. Or wait, no, she comes to when you leave, hears the door shut I suppose, and just manages to get across to the couch, and hasn't time even to put her feet up. And you want it to be a murder."

"Yes."

Durfee's voice dropped to a low, persuasive note; he gripped the edge of the desk with both hands, using self-control, and bent forward:

"Gamadge, does anybody dope a tumbler? And if so, how? Ten grains in that half pint would fix her, she'd get enough to kill her out of one good drink—she did! But that brandy in the flask *had* no poison in it. They got me definite word of that a quarter hour ago."

Gamadge did not seem to be paying much attention to this. He said: "I knew she hadn't had anything to drink before. I couldn't understand."

"Well, you understand now, don't you? But if you don't—if you still don't—" Durfee sat back. "This Iverson was calling you since one o'clock, you tell me."

"He was."

"Calling you up to explain about those papers, which were none of your business anyway. He was calling you up before you ever heard of Mrs. Wakes. Get that? Before you ever heard of her."

"I'd heard of her."

"Before you knew where she was or anything about her and you only found her this afternoon by chance."

"Well, not exactly chance."

"Inspiration, then, when you saw that name Weekes."

"Call it that," said Gamadge.

"Whatever it was, she couldn't have let them know you were coming to see her, even if she'd had a telephone. And by the time you left, she was dying."

"That's so."

"And what's more, Iverson and Mrs. Paul Bradlock didn't know you'd ever heard of her, didn't know you were looking for her, and didn't know you'd find her. So why murder her, even if she knows *they* killed Paul Bradlock? They never murdered her before. Why do it now, when the picture hasn't changed, so far as they know, at all? Besides . . ." Durfee bent forward again, this time with his forefinger pointing at Gamadge's face: "This afternoon, to hear you tell it, they give you a motive! They get you up there and give you their motive for killing Bradlock! They tell you that something valuable was found—after he died, of course—and that they sold it for a hundred thousand dollars. You think they're crazy?"

"I don't, no. What they told me doesn't constitute a motive for killing Bradlock."

"It doesn't?"

"No. It wasn't true. That manuscript they talked about was never found by Paul Bradlock or anybody else."

"You mean there was never any such thing?"

"There was such a thing, but it's lost. It wasn't picked up by Paul Bradlock in a rummage sale, if it's escaped the attention of all the professional hunters since rare documents have been hunted for. If it has been found," said Gamadge, "then I'm the wife of Bath."

Durfee asked after a pause: "You *know* it hasn't?"

"Of course I don't know. The story can't be disproved—that's why they told it. That's why they told the other one, that thin one about the letters. Nobody can disprove any of it. They told the truth twice this afternoon," said Gamadge. "Mrs. Paul Bradlock told the truth when she said she wanted to stay on at the Bradlock studio—and Iverson told it when he said that they were confessing to that hundred thousand dollar deal because I might find out about it anyway. Mrs. Bradlock's truth was obvious—it's plain that she did want to stay on; Iverson's truth was necessary—for all they knew I had ways of discovering that Mrs. Bradlock had a private income of noble proportions, instead of being penniless."

Durfee said: "That damn rigmarole. All right, they're a couple of crooks, though I can't say they seem to have broken any laws. But now go on and tell me how they got in here and put morphia in a tumbler when Mrs. Wakes wasn't looking, and then persuaded her to pour brandy in on top of the morphia later on and drink it. How could anybody count on her doing such a thing, even if she was blind and couldn't see the stuff? As for pouring out a shot of brandy and leaving it for her to drink some time or other, she just might notice that tube of morphia laying there. A perfect suicide picture, and you want to make it a murder because you don't like this Iverson. I tell you if it was murder the morphia would have been in the bottle."

"But then everybody would have known it was murder, Durfee."

Durfee opened his mouth, looked at Gamadge, and closed his mouth again.

Gamadge smiled for the first time. "You get it."

"No, I don't get it."

"Of course you get it. The poison was in the flask."

"It wasn't."

Gamadge sat up and lighted a cigarette. He said: "There was plenty of time after I left at four o'clock, before I got back at six, to come and remove the doped flask and substitute another."

"They didn't know you'd ever been here," said Durfee in a low voice.

"That's so. But *I* knew where *they* were between four and six—at the studio. They couldn't have got here after that before I did."

Durfee said slowly: "You mean they wanted you there for an alibi."

"Their alibi was good from four o'clock on; I had notice to come and find them there. They must think they have some other effective alibi up to four o'clock; after four they have a corker—me."

"And as soon as you actually came they sent somebody over to change the brandy flasks? Why not before?"

"They must have known she wouldn't start drinking till she quit work. They'd give her at least an hour to die in."

Durfee put up his hands again, this time to wave them in the air. "Gamadge, it's a pipe dream. You think they sent this little cousin over to change those flasks—the girl that beat it as soon as you got there. Or that fellow Welsh?"

"If it was Welsh he must have been hanging around outside watching for me to come, because I don't think there's a back way out of that annex. No reason why there should be."

"It's a pipe dream. The party would have had to have a key to get in. They'd have had to know all about the dead woman's habits, the fact that she took her brandy neat and drank alone, the fact that there wasn't another bottle of liquor in the place. And I ask you, does that sound like a heavy drinker—one half pint of brandy on the premises? In spite of what that super says! Take one drink and let him smell it, and that character would say anything. And there wasn't a sign she took drugs." Durfee drummed on the desk with all ten fingers. "They'll find out later, but there wasn't a sign. She had that morphia ready for the day she decided to quit."

"I'm glad you know where it came from."

"You came here, got talking about old times, and she couldn't stand it—woman who'd lost money, come down in the world. The papers are going to put it down as a plain honest-to-God suicide."

"The papers will have enough in them to suit me." Gamadge smiled.

"You mean you're satisfied to leave it that way?" Durfee looked relieved. "You're wise. All it would do would be to make a lot of trouble for those poor unfortunate Avery Bradlocks. It isn't as if there was one atom of evidence." He scowled at Gamadge again. "It's all conjecture."

Gamadge laughed. "That's what I say when you rebuke me for keeping things to myself. Don't blame me this time."

"You're going on with it?"

"Well, of course I am. I'm rather involved."

"Personally, I wouldn't know where to start." Durfee got up. "Tell you what I'll do, I'll find out if any of the neighbours saw any of these people going in here or coming out between four and six to-day."

"Thanks very much." Gamadge slowly pushed himself to his feet.

"Just try not to drive anybody else to killing themselves, that's all." Durfee walked to the door and opened it.

"I'll try." Gamadge went through into the hall. Durfee locked the door after them. "Like to bet you we don't find out anything more about this suicide," he said. "Like to bet nobody saw anybody interesting around here this afternoon?"

"No use losing my money."

"Well," said Durfee as they went downstairs, "you might keep me posted. I'm interested."

"That's good."

They went down the echoing stairs, and out into waning afternoon sunlight. Eyeing each other with friendly cynicism, they shook hands. Durfee went on down to the subway; Gamadge crossed the street and entered a drugstore. In the telephone booth he got out his notebook and looked up a number. He dialled.

A well-remembered voice came over the wire, a voice with a squeak in it: "Indus speaking."

"Thank goodness I caught you. This is—"

"Don't have to tell me that. It's Mr. Gamadge, and how are you?"

"Indus, you know everything. I'm fine, Indus. Listen, I know you retired. How do you like it, by the way?"

"Mr. Gamadge, the days ain't long enough."

"That's good hearing. You wouldn't do a little job for me, would you? It's so confidential I couldn't ask another soul."

"Mr. Gamadge, the truth is I'm past it. I couldn't foller a baby carriage, if the nurse had any kind of a stride. It's my jernts."

"I know, Indus, but you're not laid up, are you?"

"I'm brisk; it's just that I don't get around fast. Not fast enough to get out of sight in a hurry, or run for cabs."

"You could almost do this sitting down."

"What is it?"

"I want a private word or two with a young lady. She lives with a cousin in a private house, no servants, and if I could catch her when the other woman was out . . . There's a boarder, too."

"I could hang around."

"There's a drugstore around the corner from the place, on Madison. You could call me when the coast seemed to be clear."

"Is it urgent?"

"It's urgent, but we can't exactly hurry it, can we?"

"I don't know." Indus paused, then went on: "It's eight o'clock. I could start tonight—don't mind late hours. In fact, I was going to the movies."

"Well, that's so, the other woman might go out. If you got up there in a hurry—take a cab." Gamadge described the studio, and gave Indus a carefully detailed picture of the little pink-nosed girl, of Mrs. Paul Bradlock, of young Welsh and of Iverson.

"Leave it to me," said Indus. "I'll knock off at ten, call you tomorrow morning if there's nothing going on tonight."

"I'll be home myself in half an hour," said Gamadge. "Ring me any time."

He went out and looked down the avenue. A few doors below the drugstore he had noticed a liquor store, and a white-coated clerk or proprietor standing on the street and looking at the Wakes's apartment across the way. He was still there, still looking. Gamadge approached, paused, and said: "I'd like a fifth of White Label."

"Yes, sir." The clerk followed him into the store and went behind the counter. He was a little pasty man, solemn of face and very polite. He took down a bottle while Gamadge, leaning on the counter, looked at the half pints of brandy ranged on the shelves in front of a mirror.

The little man wrapped the bottle, "I saw you coming out of that apartment house," he said, "with the cop."

"Yes, I was there. I found her."

"You did!"

"Yes, awfully sad."

"Terrible," said the clerk, his round face cast down. "I wouldn't have said she'd do that."

"Nor I neither." There was a silence while the clerk wrapped the bottle. Looking up, he asked: "You a writer, too?"

"Sort of one. I was here earlier this afternoon; did you see me then?"

"Oh no, normally I wouldn't notice anybody. All those stores under the building, and that library—people go in and out of there till nine o'clock."

"That's so." Gamadge took the package and offered a bill. While the clerk made change, he said: "I never could understand why she bought her liquor in half pints."

The clerk turned. "Well, I'll tell you what I think about that. Up to a couple of years ago she drank whisky, bought it in fifths like anybody else, wouldn't use up a fifth in two weeks. But then she began to drink pretty regular, and she asked for it in half pints."

"Why, I wonder?"

The clerk handed Gamadge his change. "I told her whisky don't come in half pints. State law. So then she said—you know that tough way she had, only not tough either, she was a lady. I liked Mrs. Weekes," said the clerk earnestly.

"Yes."

"She said well, she'd lived in France long enough to get used to brandy, and she'd take half pints of brandy. From that time forth, she came in here every evening after supper, and she got her half pint; absolute routine."

"Half a pint of brandy a day! That's plenty."

"You'd be surprised. They get a tolerance."

"After supper, you say? Then she'd have it to go to sleep on, and perhaps a little left over for tomorrow."

"She never took a drop till she quit work and then just a shot or two, the way somebody else would have a cup of tea."

"Little stimulant, of course. Did you say you doped out why she made the switch?"

"I think I did." The clerk put his elbows on the counter and clasped his hands. He rubbed his thumbs together thoughtfully. "A half pint goes into a lady's handbag."

"So it does."

"She could carry it home or anywhere, and after it was empty she could drop it in a rubbish can. A half pint doesn't show up, full or empty, the way a fifth does. Easy to dispose of. I bet the police didn't find any empties up there."

"No, they didn't."

"Did she—did she take the stuff in brandy?"

"Yes, she did. Took one shot, or so they think, and there was a little left in the bottle."

The clerk nodded sadly. "That would be just about what she'd have left for the afternoon."

"She didn't offer me a drink while I was there."

"I bet she didn't?"

"Financial reasons?"

"That, I guess, but also they like to think nobody knows." He added: "Nobody did know but me. As you said, it was just to go to sleep on."

But the superintendent had known. Two years—that was a long time to keep a secret; perhaps the shot in the afternoon gave her away.

"She was a funny character," said the clerk. "Full of fight, she'd raise the dickens if she tripped over somebody's dog or some man tried to get in ahead of her with his order here. But always pleasant to me, and lots to talk about every evening. 'How's your business to-day,' she'd say, 'mine is rotten.'"

"She worked hard."

"I guess—living alone, business bad—she had some excuse for drinking."

"She must have had some excuse, yes."

Gamadge took his bottle and rode home.

# 13

# Night Life

By nine o'clock the Gamadges were nearing the end of their dinner, at the round table beside the window in the library. Malcolm was announced, came in, and said with an avid look at Gamadge that he had come for coffee.

"Yes, and for news," said Clara. "Perhaps he'll give you some. It must be very bad, because he has that gloomy look and won't open his mouth except to eat."

"And drink." Gamadge swallowed whisky.

"He's been drinking whisky right through dinner," said Clara.

"To tell you the truth I came for whisky," said Malcolm, sitting down next to Clara. "I thought you'd be done with dinner long ago."

"We never sat down until twenty minutes to nine. I don't know where he was."

Gamadge said: "Tell you all about it later. I may have to go out again, and if anybody rings up and asks questions you can say you don't know anything about it or where I am."

"And how true that will be."

"And they'll know it's true. The mildest prevarication," said Gamadge, "and you stammer and stutter."

"Can't you teach her to do better than that?" Malcolm was eyeing Gamadge with ill-concealed impatience.

"No, she won't learn."

The telephone in the hall rang, and Gamadge took it.

The voice of Indus sounded jubilant: "Mr. Gamadge, I got her isolated."

"No!"

"We're at the movies, Translux at Eighty-fifth and Madison. She and this feller Welsh went to the nine o'clock pictures, they're lookin' at it now, and I'm downstairs in the lounge telephoning. The picture lasts till ten-thirty, and you say he has to be at the hospital at eleven. But I thought she might not leave with him, because they missed the newsreel and the cartoon, and she might stay on and see them. It's a Disney."

"Not such a long shot, Indus. I'll be there."

"Even if she did go to the hospital with him—it ain't much of a walk—she'd have to come home alone afterwards."

"That's so."

"I'll be standing up at the back, where I can keep watching them. I'll point 'em out when you get here. When he goes you might get a chance at his seat. There's not such a crowd for the last show."

"I'll be up in good time."

"No hurry, it's a good picture, and they paid for it. They're set till ten-thirty."

Gamadge went back into the library. "I find I do have to go out again in a little while. Dave, what about having that drink in the office?"

Clara said: "Isn't he wonderful, the way he saves me worry? Here's coffee; or do you want yours down in the office too?"

They had coffee together, and then Gamadge and Malcolm went down in the little elevator, leaving Clara hunched up with a cat on her knee, glumly watching them go.

Down in the office Malcolm sat listening in consternation while Gamadge related the events of the afternoon. At the end of the recital he composed himself with most of his highball. Then he asked: "You mean Durfee didn't see any tie-up at all?"

"It all hangs on the substitution of the flasks, and Durfee didn't get all the details about the letters and *The*

*Book of the Lion* into his head." Gamadge laughed shortly. "Even if he had, he might not have caught the implications."

"Why did they get you there this afternoon and tell you that stuff? Just to prove *they* couldn't have changed the flasks? As Durfee said, they didn't even know you ever heard the name of Wakes, much less Weekes."

"I got that police detail about the apartment house; that never was published—they didn't know the police ever had it."

"Well, then, why bother about an alibi for your benefit?"

"Suppose the papers publish her real name and connect her with Paul Bradlock's past in France? They may. Then mightn't I begin to make a nuisance of myself again? But if I did, I'd find out that Mrs. Wakes never took a drink until four o'clock, when Iverson and Mrs. Paul Bradlock were safely holed up in the studio expecting me at any minute. One of them could have doped her own half pint any time to-day; it's obvious that Iverson or Vera Bradlock— probably Vera Bradlock—knew her well. There must have been a key—stolen?"

"*They* knew she didn't drink until four o'clock . . . Who's the accomplice? You don't send a messenger boy to change brandy flasks, with a woman dead in the room. Who was it?"

"I'd like to find out."

"The cousin? The Welsh boy? Both dependents. Great Moses I'd like to see their reaction when they read the papers tomorrow morning! They'll get the news that you'd found out who she was and had gone to see her earlier, and that you actually discovered the body. And you hadn't said a word about her when you were at the studio this afternoon! They'll hit the ceiling. You were miles ahead of them."

"They were miles ahead of me." Gamadge looked up at Malcolm somberly. "They didn't wait for me to find her, Dave."

"Well, what is it all about? I suppose they did kill Paul Bradlock, for something of value that he got from Mrs. Wakes that evening; it certainly wasn't on him when he was found dead. Two years later, when they think Mrs. Wakes may be drawn into it and give them away, she's killed too. That right?"

"It may be."

"Mrs. Wakes took to brandy about the time Bradlock was killed."

"There's that too."

"You say Bradlock wasn't killed for the Chaucer manuscript, because there was no Chaucer manuscript."

"No. Tell that story to Avery Bradlock? I wouldn't tell it as fact to anybody," said Gamadge. "But they had to tell me something, to account for Mrs. Paul's financial situation, and I certainly can't disprove what they said. Nobody could."

"They must have cooked it up around Eigenstern's crash. Fitted right in."

Gamadge said: "They sold something of value; if not *The Book of the Lion*, what was it? They told me she pretended there were letters so that she could stay on at the studio and write a book. She undoubtedly wanted to stay on at the studio, but not for that reason. Whether they killed Paul Bradlock for the equivalent of a fortune, or whether they found the valuable property later, she had it; she didn't need to stay, and there seems to be no reason why she should have stayed. But she wanted to."

"That's evident."

Gamadge stood up and looked down at his friend. "They told me a lot of things, Dave, but one of the things was something they didn't mean to tell. Now if you've finished your drink, I'm sorry, but I have to go."

"Where?"

"To the movies."

"All right, I won't ask any more questions."

"I wouldn't know the answers."

On the doorstep, still longing for information, Malcolm hesitated. He said: "I'm glad if you have a line on them. It would be a little too tough to see them get away with two murders and a hundred thousand dollars."

"I think so myself. I'm not sure I have a line on them, Dave."

"Go and meditate at the movies."

Malcolm turned right at Lexington Avenue, Gamadge went on to Madison. The Madison Avenue bus took him slowly, with swoops and halts, jerks and starts, to Eighty-fourth Street. He got out, crossed, and walked up to the Translux.

The posters outside confirmed his forebodings—his taste and Indus's taste were not the same. He hoped that the quarry within had not got up and left, disgusted by this preposterous romance, which even Theodore, who was sentimental, had warned him against. He bought a ticket and went in, past the lobby, to darkness. He dropped his ticket in the box, and walked on. He found Indus leaning against the rail, submerged in unearthly light.

They shook hands; Indus muttered: "Down there, tenth row, third and fourth seats in. Big feller; she has some kind of flowers on her head, sort of a hat."

"I see them. Thanks, Indus."

"There's an empty seat along this back row."

"I see it."

"Want me any more?"

"I'll call you."

"Like old times, ain't it?" The squirrel face of Indus wore its driest smile.

"Don't know what I would have done if you hadn't—"

"Glad to oblige."

Indus melted into the shades. Gamadge went forward, insinuated himself into the empty seat, and was about to close his eyes and slumber, when he realized that he couldn't do that. Sunk in unutterable gloom he watched the pair in the tenth row, while voices from the screen assaulted his ears and figures loomed and vanished on the edge of his vision.

At last the screen was blank, and the lights came up. Were those two going? No. Welsh was going, but alone. Sally would get her money's worth.

The young man, looking very big in his slacks and sports jacket, lumbered down the aisle and across to an exit door beside the proscenium. Gamadge waited until the lights dimmed, and then sidled into his place. His neighbour, engrossed by coming attractions, paid no attention to him. She had powdered the turned-up nose and put lipstick on her mouth. In her thin suit and little flowery hat she was a wisp.

Gamadge waited until the newsreel was well on its way. Then he murmured in her ear: "Isn't it Mrs. Bradlock's cousin?"

She turned, and gave him a blank look.

"My name's Gamadge. I—"

Her face was transfigured by a radiant smile—the first he had seen on it. She said: "Of course I remember! It was just that I didn't know you at first in this light—and it's such a surprise."

"I dropped in for the newsreel, and I saw you down here with an empty seat beside you."

"Tom Welsh was with me. He's just gone." She seemed delighted by this encounter. "I always like it to have somebody with me at the movies, it's so much more fun."

"Much."

"I'm sorry you missed the picture."

Somebody shushed her angrily. They exchanged guilty smiles, and concentrated on the screen. She reacted thoroughly to each event, now and then nudging him in the ribs with a thin elbow, once, at a great moment of excitement and noise, even snatching at his hand. Occasionally they exchanged a glance of sympathy or disapproval. The little cousin was not *blasé*.

When the reel ended, Gamadge said: "I don't know how you feel, but I'd like a snack somewhere. Do you absolutely have to see the cartoon?"

"Oh, I'd rather go with you."

They made their way to the aisle, and out by the exit that Welsh had used. Standing in the dark reaches of Eighty-fifth Street, she said: "I come here all the time. Do you?"

"No, it's pretty far up town for me. I really don't know my way about the neighbourhood well. Any place you prefer to go for a sandwich and a beer, or something?"

"There's a nice place on Lexington that Tom and I go to."

"Fine, we'll get a cab at the corner."

"Oh, we don't need a cab. It isn't far."

Turning pleased glances up to him, she trotted at his side. They walked east along Eighty-fifth. "You know," said Gamadge, "it's ridiculous, but I have no idea what your name is, Miss Sally."

"It's Orme."

"That Mrs. Bradlock's name, too?"

"No, hers was Larkin. We came from the same place— a little town west of Minneapolis called Summerville. Wasn't she wonderful to just leave everything and go to Paris?"

"Enterprising."

"She just wouldn't stay in Summerville."

"Neither would you."

"Oh, but I had nobody left there belonging to me. I was all alone, too. So I took what money I had and came here to business school. I copy manuscripts for people now, it's very interesting. Soon I may be able to support myself entirely. The agency gives me so much to do."

"Did you copy manuscript for your distinguished relative Paul Bradlock?"

"Oh, no; I didn't come to the studio to live until he was dead."

"Your friend Mr. Welsh from the old town, too?"

"No, I met him when I was working at night in the U.S.O."

"And introduced him to your cousin?"

"Yes, I used to bring him to see Vera sometimes— before Mr. Bradlock died. And then afterwards, when I came there to live, and he was out of hospital, he came too." She added, looking up at Gamadge: "We don't just live on her, Mr. Gamadge. We do the work."

"All of it?"

"Oh, yes. For our board. We're awfully lucky to be there."

"Mrs. Bradlock is considerably lucky to have you. A couple comes high these days."

"It's awfully good of her to have us there in that nice house."

"Only of course it's Mr. Avery Bradlock's, isn't it?"

"Yes. I suppose so. I always think of it as Vera's."

"I'm sure he does, too."

They crossed Lexington and turned south. She said: "It isn't as if Tommy could really support himself yet. He was in the merchant service and torpedoed. His father died while he was at sea, and he has no money. He can't do his own work yet."

"What does he want to do?"

"He was up at Columbia studying to be a metallurgist . . . He's very strong physically now, but if he has to work *for* anything—I mean examinations and tests, you know—he gets so tired."

"Do they think he'll soon be able to try it again?"

Her face was anxious. "Yes, they hope so. It makes him very restless."

"No wonder Mrs. Bradlock is interested in him."

"She thinks a lot of Tommy. Once when we were there—before Mr. Bradlock died—" she broke off to look up at Gamadge. "Do you *know* about Mr. Bradlock, Mr. Gamadge?"

"I know a good deal, yes."

"We never went to the studio to see Vera when he was at home. He was always out in the evenings, you know; he came back very late."

"So I understand."

"Once he came back early, and we heard him—" She paused, as if overwhelmed by memory. "We heard him coming along the flagged walk. Vera jumped up, we could hear him laughing and shouting and singing. Tom went out, and found him lying—lying—" She went hurriedly on: "Tom got him in, and it was terrible. Terrible. And Vera might have been alone, she often was. I don't know how she lived. Tom said he was dangerous."

"I suppose Mrs. Paul knew how to handle it, or she couldn't have gone on with it."

"After that, once or twice, she called Tommy and he went out with her and looked for Mr. Bradlock and brought him home. They knew just where to go."

"That was something, anyhow."

She stopped as they reached a basement bar and grill, down a flight of steps from the pavement. "Here we are."

It was a clean, neat place, lighted by a bleak bluish glare. A radio moaned quietly to itself, invisible. There were no other customers; the barman greeted Miss Orme condescendingly, as an old acquaintance. He cast a sly glance at Gamadge.

"It's all right," Gamadge told him. "I'm just a stand-in."

"I wondered where the boy-friend was."

"I guess I can have more than one," said Miss Orme, pleased with this humour. "I met an awfully nice boy at business school," she informed Gamadge. "He has a very good position in a bank now."

"More the better," said the barman. "Do 'em good."

They sat at a table below the window, where they could look out at the dark and quiet avenue. Now and then a bus went by, now and then a cab. The barman placed their order—beer and cheese sandwiches, Miss Orme's choice— on the checked cloth.

"Isn't it nice here?" She was in high spirits.

"Very cheerful. I'm glad you got over your cold. Is it pretty damp in that studio?"

"Well, it is, when the furnace isn't on. It's heated from the other house, and I don't think it ever was very warm in the annex. It wasn't meant to be lived in, you know."

"I should think Mrs. Bradlock would have fires; keep the cook-general on her feet." Gamadge took a bite of fluffy bread and processed cheese. He washed it down with beer.

"Well, we do have fires in the evening if it's cold."

"And Mr. Welsh is tucked up in bed."

"He isn't there half long enough, I think."

Miss Orme was working on her sandwich with every indication of enjoyment. Gamadge asked: "What's the layout of the place?"

"Just two little bedrooms upstairs off the gallery, they used to be cloakrooms, and a bath. There's a kitchen and another bathroom downstairs off the living-room. Vera sleeps down there on the couch. She likes it—she says it's airier."

"And it must have been more convenient, when Bradlock was alive."

"Poor Vera."

"Where do you go when they have a business conference and throw you out—as they did last night and this afternoon?"

She laughed. "I just take a walk or do shopping or go to the movies."

"Why not up to your room for a rest?"

"Those rooms are so small and stuffy."

"Just holes to crawl into. No back door to dive out of in an emergency?"

"Oh, no."

"What's it like in the back? I couldn't see from the street. Somebody's garden?"

"I don't know. There aren't any windows in the back. Our bedroom windows look out on the wall of the house next door."

"Alley there?"

"No, it's just a space, closed off."

"Well, you're very snug." Gamadge's sandwich was already lying heavy on his chest. He asked: "You never really met the Avery Bradlocks until last night? There's a wonderful-looking woman!"

"Oh, isn't she? But she looks so frozen. No, I never met them before. They never come." She puzzled over this, her eyes on her glass of beer, her hand clasping it.

"And you never go."

"They ask Vera to dinner sometimes; Christmas and Easter. I don't think relatives by marriage always do care much about one another, do you, Mr. Gamadge?" Her eyes questioned him candidly.

"Cousins don't either."

After a moment she said: "Vera's very nice to get on with. I didn't think I spoke as if I didn't like her."

"You didn't. She doesn't impress me as your type, that's all."

"Tom likes her."

"That's lucky. Isn't there a friend of Mrs. Bradlock's that she sees a good deal of—a Mrs. Wakes, Weekes?"

"I don't think I ever heard of her. Vera never knew many people here in New York. She couldn't."

"I suppose not. Bradlock would break up any party, I should think."

"She couldn't go anywhere."

They smoked a cigarette, and then Gamadge paid and they went out into the bleakness of the street. This time Gamadge hailed a cab, and they rode home in style. Once, turning to Gamadge, that radiant smile on her face, she said: "I love to ride."

"That's good."

"I enjoyed the evening so much."

"It would be nice to meet again. My wife would like to make your acquaintance, Sally. Would you have time to drop in some day?"

"Oh, I'd love to. I'd love to come."

"Here's the address. Any day, the sooner the better. We have tea in the afternoons. Mr. Iverson thinks it's rather sissy, but I always slop mine in the saucer—if that makes it less so."

"I love tea."

"Like cats? We have a couple, and a dog. There's a little boy, but he isn't allowed to pester visitors."

"I don't know any families. I'd *love* to come."

They turned into the Bradlocks' street, and Gamadge had the driver stop at the iron gates. He got out, kept the cab, and walked down the flagged yard with Sally. He could see Paul Bradlock staggering home over those flags, past the windows of his brother's house.

She opened the door with her key and went in. Gamadge returned to his cab and gave an address. They passed a handsome car stopping at the Bradlocks'; within it Gamadge caught a glimpse of Avery Bradlock in a white tie, and Mrs. Avery Bradlock, beautiful and pale, beside him. Another life, another world.

Well, he was travelling now with a certainty; the little typist who "loved to ride," who had greeted him so radiantly in the Translux Theatre, had not been sent on that errand to the Wakes apartment at five o'clock that afternoon. Sally Orme had nothing on her mind but the struggle for existence, and the problems of her friends.

# 14

# Graveyard Stretch

The Medical and Surgical Hospital spreads its great bulk over a city block, new brick and stone buildings stemming out from old. Gamadge paid off the cab and walked up broad steps between bronze lanterns. He pushed open a bronze door and then a glass one that led from the vestibule into the great white corridor.

An office window on his right was empty. He pushed a muted bell, and the receptionist came out of her inner sanctum and looked at him. She was a tall dark girl, who had not bothered to make up for the long hours of the night.

Gamadge leaned on the window ledge, all humility.

"I don't know whether I'm asking too much," he said. "If there's a rule, tell me."

The young lady looked as if there were a good many rules, if she cared to remember them. She asked: "What was it?"

"You have an orderly here on night duty, man named Welsh. Do you think I could speak to him?"

The receptionist looked blank.

"Tell you how it is," said Gamadge. "I didn't know how to get hold of him any other way—this is the only address I have. It's about a job for him. You know his history, of course—he was a patient here. War hero."

"I know him."

"Well, we all want to give him a hand. A part-time job, morning or afternoon, in his own line of work—it might help out, till he's ready to go on with his work at the University."

"I don't know whether he's available. You might go and sit down in the waiting-room over there, while I inquire."

"Mighty nice of you. Here's my card."

Gamadge crossed to the waiting-room, and sat in a wooden armchair beside a table. After a wait, a man in a business suit came to the door and looked at him. He said: "Mr. Gamadge? I'm the night supervisor."

Gamadge rose. "Oh yes. About Mr. Welsh?"

The supervisor came into the waiting-room. Gamadge's card in his hand. He looked at it. "We'd like to know something about this job, Mr. Gamadge. Welsh—being our patient, we ought to know what he'd be getting into."

Gamadge explained himself and his work. "It just struck me that a little laboratory work with me might be the very thing for this boy. No responsibility, and surroundings he'd feel at home in. I wouldn't suggest it, but I understand he *is* doing some daytime work, perhaps not entirely congenial. I could give you references. Dr. Ethelbert Hamish, and others."

The supervisor said: "It sounds as if it might be what he needs—get him into line again. He's not a psychoneurotic case, Mr. Gamadge. He was under a long nervous strain, and it's left him with a certain lack of self-confidence. That's all. He's been afraid to tackle anything that entails— afraid to fail, you know." The supervisor's spectacles glinted in the bare light.

"I understand perfectly. I'd do the paper work. Could I see him?"

"Well, I'd better speak to him first. Are you prepared to wait until he's at liberty? And there might be a call for him at any moment. He's on duty for ambulance cases tonight."

"Glad to wait, of course."

The supervisor went away. Gamadge sat down again and lighted a cigarette. In perhaps ten minutes Welsh appeared in the doorway, looking very big, clumsy, and dark in his whites. He stood for a moment glowering; then he said: "I ought to sock you."

"Sock me? For offering you this job?"

"Vera's been telling me," said Welsh in an angry voice.

"Telling you to sock me? Well, I'm not entirely surprised at that," said Gamadge.

Welsh came forward and stood looking down at Gamadge, his big hands clenched. He said: "You think it's so unethical for her to put up that game on Avery Bradlock—about those letters. I carried them down to Iverson's place and up to his room, and let me tell you I'd have been tickled to death to do it if I'd known the box was full of old newspapers. Glad she was smart enough to do it, and it was none of your damn business."

Gamadge said mildly: "Not knowing the parties well, I can't be blamed for wondering whether Mr. Iverson mightn't be putting something over on her. Or can I?"

Welsh, taken aback, gazed at him frowning. Then he said: "I didn't get the impression you were on her side. My God, when I think of those Bradlocks in their house—guzzling and swilling."

Gamadge raised his eyebrows. "You've seen them at it?"

"I don't have to."

"Mr. Avery Bradlock can hardly be blamed for eating and drinking under his own roof. Does he ration *you*?"

Welsh, rigid, his head a little forward, colour coming up on his cheekbones, was silent.

"Sorry for the allusion," said Gamadge amiably, "but I don't understand this resentment against Mr. Bradlock, just because he pays the bills. If he covers the expenses of three people instead of merely his sister-in-law's, that's his business. He knows what they are."

Welsh said with repressed fury: "I eat out."

"No doubt you do. You're quite justified in feeling sympathy for Mrs. Paul Bradlock, Mr. Welsh, and for excusing her little game about the letters. Would you feel as sympathetic if you knew that she had sold property of her husband's soon after his death, and that she is now enjoying an income from the proceeds—an income on one hundred thousand dollars?"

Welsh stared. "Who told you so?"

"She did. Iverson did. I'm not surprised that they didn't tell you about *The Book of the Lion*."

"The what?"

Gamadge laughed. "A fable. I had the pleasure of a

short visit with your friend Miss Orme this evening." He
looked Welsh in the eye. "Get her out of there."

"What?"

"Get her out of that place, Welsh."

The young man, looking bewildered, came up and
leaned against the table; he said: "I don't know what you
mean. We owe Vera—"

"You don't owe her a damned thing."

"How can I—why should I get Sally away from Vera
Bradlock?"

"Because she doesn't belong there. You think it's all
right for Mrs. Paul Bradlock to lie herself out of the holes
she gets into, and play these tricks on her brother-in-law;
can you imagine Sally Orme doing it?

"If you call her a little woman," said Gamadge
violently, "I'll sock *you*. And I could last several rounds,
believe it or not."

Welsh, completely bemused, glanced at Gamadge's
length and build and said nothing.

"Sally Orme," continued Gamadge, "is a rare type—
candid and kind. Do you like Iverson?"

"Just a city feller," muttered Welsh.

"So am I; do I remind you of him?"

There was a silence. Then Welsh said: "I couldn't even
take care of her."

"She could take care of herself. She's staying at the
studio because she thinks she's needed; she'd get full-time
work tomorrow. As for you, I'm offering you the chance to
get a room of your own."

Welsh asked: "You know I'm not even a chemist yet?"

"You'll do. I have a queer profession, Mr. Welsh, as
you probably know, and I don't punch clocks on my assistants. There's a lot of photographic enlargement involved in
the work I do, analysis of inks and paper, that kind of thing.
You'd soon get the idea. If I need highly expert work I get it
from a regular technician. Most men in your field are full-
time workers, and I don't need that. I want somebody who
can find his way around a laboratory, and can use apparatus."

Welsh said after a pause: "I'd like the job, if—" he put

his hand up and rubbed the back of his head. "Have to look it over."

"It'll pay your rent, at least, and you can work it in with this job for the time being."

"I catch up on sleep in the mornings, if I can."

"Suits me. How about coming in tomorrow afternoon, just after lunch? And you might ask Miss Orme to drop in for tea. She's already accepted the invitation for some day unspecified."

Welsh's eyes roved around the white room. "I'd have to speak to Vera Bradlock."

"Naturally. Did they give you that card of mine? No? Well, here's another, and here"—Gamadge scribbled on it—"is my telephone number." He rose. "Think it over."

Welsh said slowly: "Thanks."

Gamadge left him standing with the card in his hand, and went out and through the bronze doors to the front steps. He decided to walk the half mile home.

This might be the last night for some time that he would feel entirely free to walk deserted streets so late. He smiled. The deadline! Tomorrow morning there would be the news in the papers that he had been trespassing again. Too bad that young Mr. Welsh couldn't be hired as a bodyguard.

Gamadge was now approaching a stretch on Lexington, opposite the old Armoury, that is peculiarly dark and quiet at night, almost utterly so in the small hours. It was on this stretch that he first asked himself exactly why he thought he could set a deadline for Mrs. Paul Bradlock and Mr. Hilliard Iverson. They hadn't waited for him to find Mrs. Wakes before they killed her; they hadn't waited until he knew she was dead, to inform him by implication that they couldn't be responsible. Why should they wait for the morning papers before making a try at eliminating the only human being who seemed likely to be in the slightest degree dangerous to them? Since they had seen him in the afternoon he had had private talk with Sally Orme, and she might easily have reported it. He had had private talk of a most explosive character with Thomas Welsh, and he might not wait until morning before reporting to Vera Bradlock—

there were certainly telephones at the hospital. What more likely? Loyal young people both.

And if Welsh had reported, Iverson—or Mrs. Bradlock, for that matter, Gamadge wouldn't put it past her— could get to his street before he did. A dark, quiet residential street, with plenty of cover for all.

No cabs anywhere. By the time Gamadge reached his corner he was entirely convinced that some deep area-way contained somebody with a blunt instrument. They wouldn't shoot, they hated a noise. Damn it all, he thought, annoyed with himself for this onslaught of nerves, he couldn't run.

He swung into the block. There were the two rows of unlighted private houses, the wells of darkness between. Trees to make it more shadowy, a tree in fact obscuring the one street light. Half-way down the block a figure moved— two figures, one of them curiously dwarfed. Something a little like a lion? He recognized his wife Clara, hatless and in her topcoat, walking her chow.

Gamadge, smiling, stopped to contemplate this heartening vision. Once he had seen a man fall to his death before the rush of that tawny catapult. He laughed, walking forward. There was a deafening bark, and Clara turned, waved, slipped the leash. Sun leapt to meet him, stood up and put his paws on Gamadge's shoulders. Gamadge embraced the huge furry head; he greeted Clara as sternly as he could:

"May I ask what you mean by being out on the streets at this hour?"

"You know I'm all right with Sun. I thought I'd wait up, and why shouldn't we come out for a breath of air?"

Sun, who had dropped to four feet, looked up at Gamadge with his black tongue hanging out. Gamadge said: "Why shouldn't you? Any prowlers?"

"Prowlers? No. Just a minute ago a man did come into the block from Third, but Sun let out such a horrible growl that he went away. We'll be fined if he barks and growls at people like that."

"I'll pay his fine. Do you realize that even if somebody

shot at you, they couldn't get away afterwards? He'd get them and tear them to bits."

"I suppose he would. No, Sun, you know you're not allowed near the tree. Let's go in." As Gamadge unlocked the door, she added: "I suppose I'm not to ask where you've been."

Gamadge turned to her and laughed: "You and Sun saved my life and reason. I'd as soon keep the Marines out of it!"

# 15

## Expert

J. Hall, dealer in rare books, had practically retired; but he maintained the two rooms, on the second floor of a converted private house in the Forties, which he used as an office and stockroom. The room in the rear had a fireplace; and here he sat, looking over old catalogues and making notes for the book he was going to write some day, while the world rumbled beyond his philosophy. He watched the change of seasons as it manifested itself through the sycamore tree in his back yard.

To-day, at mid-morning, he looked up testily when Albert, his clerk, opened the sliding doors, and peered through.

"It's Mr. Gamadge, sir."

"Oh. Well. Send him in. How are you?" asked Hall, as Gamadge appeared. "Come in and sit down. How's your wife?"

"Splendid." Gamadge sank into the leather chair opposite his host. "Hope you'll be coming up to dinner soon."

"Glad to. Now that's a woman."

"She loves your stories. By the way, I've come to hear one."

"Of course you have. You never do come unless you want something. What is it this time?"

"I want to know about literary forgers in Paris in the twenties. Wasn't there a regular ring?"

J. Hall looked up at him sharply. "Now how did you hear about that? It wasn't broadcast."

"Some people showed me a description of what purported to be a newly discovered manuscript. It was perfectly done, must have been done by an expert in such things."

"Well, what of it?" asked Hall.

"I got an idea that it was done in Paris in the twenties. One of the crowd must have been a scholar. One or more of them found old stuff to imitate—in libraries or old country houses in England. Then there were the artists who actually did the work. There must have been a lot of research done." Gamadge sat back and put his fingertips together. "This is between us; there was a little man named Wakes."

Hall said after a moment: "If we're going to mention names, there was a woman named Mrs. Wakes, and a man named Brandon. He was the scholar involved."

"I imagined so."

"Truth is," said Hall, his eyes on the distant branches of the sycamore, "except for poor Brandon no names got out past a few people that didn't want publicity. Brandon killed himself, and the thing was allowed to drop. Wakes died—of fright, I suppose. His widow came back to America and disappeared. You understand, the few people in the know made it plain that if there wasn't a complete scattering and cessation, they'd bring charges; but nobody wants to bring charges if they can help it, because—we—" Hall smiled. "They may have bought stuff themselves."

"Good as that, was it?"

"Couldn't be better. In those days people weren't alerted as they've been since the thirties, you know—to paper and so on; but I understand that Wakes managed to get some paper, flyleaves and endpapers and so on. Ever read his books? And would you believe it?"

"I suppose he'd lost his money?"

"If he ever had much. These old families—half the time you don't really know."

"Does evidence exist against these people?"

"Only some of the stuff they put out. Mrs. Wakes, clever woman, helped with the literary end of it. I don't know who half the others were, nobody does now. Probably never did. Poor Brandon, he was the goat. He'd taken to drugs, and he needed the money. Drugs made him careless, and they found faked manuscripts in his room after his death, and his notes and so on. So the police had it all, and he had to get the publicity. But he was only the adviser. Too bad."

"He'd be able to describe a lost book of Chaucer?"

"Oh, child's play for Brandon. But that would be a little too much for the most credulous amateur collector to swallow, I should say."

"The notion is fantastic, is it—finding one of the lost books now?"

Hall got out a large silk handkerchief in rich colours and rubbed his nose with it. He put it away, and asked: "Somebody trying to sell you one?"

"Not in the sense you mean. I was shown a description. The manuscript—fifteenth-century copy—is now said to be lost again, for good."

Hall said: "Let's be conservative; let's say that the big jump in values came in the last fifty years; also the big drive for manuscripts, and the intensive research. Have you any idea how many dealers, scholars, paid research experts, thesis writers and collectors have been raking over the middens in the British Isles and Europe during this last half century? Have you any idea how many of them would be Chaucerians? Do you suppose much stuff has escaped them, or that they haven't heard of the stuff that may exist but is inaccessible?"

"I didn't think myself that there was any chance of such a find."

"Finds occur. I'd say the odds against this one were astronomical. I don't know why Brandon or any other forger considered putting such a thing on the market."

"I had a kind of theory that it may have been an abandoned project."

Hall wrinkled up his face and thought this over.

"It might have tempted Brandon," continued Gamadge. "The big money in it if he could put it over. If he knew where to get the right materials, paper and vellum, and could employ an expert in fifteenth-century script; it might tempt him. Such an invention would be great fun—I'm sure somebody got a lot of fun out of doing that description."

Hall said: "But why were you supposed to swallow the description, and the story about the manuscript?"

"Well, the people who showed the description to me may not have realized how fabulous such a find as *The Book of the Lion* would be."

"I'm no Chaucerian; was that one of them?"

"Yes. All correct. I think these people may have got hold of the description somehow, at some time, probably in Paris—"

"Clever of the gang, to operate in Paris with British material."

"Very. These people I'm speaking of might have got hold of the description and Brandon's notes on it—probable market value of the fake, proper way to introduce it, plausible story of the way it was found. He might even have advised his employers to put the end page in the middle, so that it could seem to have been innocently acquired at a sale."

Hall was staring. After a pause he said: "You must meet some queer characters."

"I do. These people who tried to sell me the idea may have been on the distributing end of the game, but experts in any other way. They'd think, if they found Brandon's notes, that he must have known what he was about and that the discovery was credible." Gamadge, watching the smoke of his cigarette rise, smiled a little. "A bookstore, now—shouldn't you say that would be a good distributing centre? A bookstore in Paris. Literary characters dropping in, high thinking and small profits for enthusiasts. And then there'd be the travelling American, business man with hobbies, sociable bachelor with money in his pockets, all sympathy and comprehension. He'd distribute pretty well, too. Some such character gave me the line on the Chaucer discovery."

Hall's only comment was a kind of snort.

"Don't you think their minds might have worked in the way I suggest?" asked Gamadge. "The man called me a graphologist; that isn't what he meant, but at least it shows that he wouldn't make fine distinctions in other ways. Don't you agree with me?"

"I don't profess to follow the mental processes of such pests," said Hall with some irritation. "They drive us all crazy. I've no doubt that plenty of Brandon's middle-English masterpieces are still kicking around in dealers' safe deposit boxes, questionable for ever. Luckily Brandon didn't do much with the moderns, but others did. Those damn' Byron and Shelley letters! What a profession. The unfortunate Wakes woman, she had a good start as a writer. Now, if she's still alive, she's probably still wondering if the bolt will fall—ruin and disgrace. If Wakes hadn't died he'd have ended in jail, not a doubt of it."

"Mrs. Wakes died yesterday."

Hall peered at Gamadge. "Is that why you're here?"

"I'm here because I'm interested in that description of the Chaucer manuscript." Gamadge rose and walked over to a bookshelf.

Hall craned over the side of his armchair. "Albert! Albert! My morning paper." He resumed his sunken posture, watching Gamadge as he passed along inspecting books. "All this was twenty years ago," he said. "Everybody's dead."

"Yes. Did you ever hear of Paul Bradlock in that connection?" Gamadge pulled out a volume, examined it, put it back.

"Bradlock? Bradlock? What do you mean? His signed letters or his manuscripts aren't worth enough to interest a forger, and never were . . ." Hall struggled to a more upright position in his chair. "You mean he was a member of the ring? I never heard so." He sank back again. "Wouldn't particularly surprise me. I don't know what his morals were like when he was young, but by the time he was killed he'd sunk low. Shoddy tricks—borrowing from people who couldn't afford to lose their money, cadging from strangers." Hall looked amused. "Did he blackmail his old friends and get his head beaten in for his pains?"

Albert came in with morning papers, and Hall snatched them. Gamadge thanked him for information received, and went away in a hurry. He was not anxious to be there when Hall discovered his close involvement with Mrs. Wakes's death; he wouldn't get away for an hour, and it was getting on for lunch time.

Riding up town, he reflected that blackmail was perhaps the only way in which anybody could have profited by Mrs. Wakes; but what could Mrs. Wakes have possessed of value to a blackmailer? *She* was none—whatever she had, she never used it. And if Bradlock could use it, he himself was not implicated.

She had taken to brandy "a couple of years ago"; the inference was, about the time of Bradlock's death. Because she had been forced out of fear for her own safety to do something that made it hard for her to sleep of nights? And had Bradlock's death released the information she had given him to other, even more sinister, keeping?

At his own corner Gamadge bought a newspaper. He had already seen one, and this edition gave no further news. It said that Isabel Wakes, writing and living under the pen name of Imogen Weekes, had died of an overdose of morphia. Despondent (this favourite newspaper word had been furnished by the superintendent of her building), she had taken her own life. Mr. Henry Gamadge, writer and document expert, had been calling on her earlier that afternoon, gathering material for an article on her late husband Jeremy, and on other personalities in Paris in the 1920's. Reminiscence had probably been too much for her. Mr. Gamadge, returning by appointment at six o'clock, had found her dead.

There was further information about her career as a pulp ghost writer, and a general implication that she had had a long and bitter struggle, and had concealed it successfully from all but her agent and one or two others, business contacts. There was comment on her first book, written so long before, which had had good reviews; and on the fact that Jeremy Wakes had lost his money. That was about all.

It was enough. Gamadge tried to visualize the expressions of Iverson and Mrs. Paul Bradlock as they absorbed these paragraphs with their morning coffee.

He found Malcolm in the library, getting the news from Clara and fuming with impatience. Gamadge said he had nothing to add at present, and that he wanted his lunch.

"Nothing to add! Nothing to add!" Malcolm sat down reluctantly with the two others at the round table in the library window; a tall and wide French window, through which Gamadge had a better view of his ailanthus than Hall had of his sycamore. "I don't know why you're alive and capable of adding anything, even if you wanted to. You oughtn't to go out of the house until these people are bound over to keep the peace, or whatever it is."

"Nonsense." Gamadge had begun on his celery.

"You think so? You think I couldn't kill you any time, anywhere, and have it filed as accident?"

Clara looked up and asked, startled: "Could you, Dave?"

"Of course I could. And they're professionals."

"Nonsense," repeated Gamadge. "They can't do that now. You forget—they've read the papers. Even Durfee would tie it up now."

"And you've gone and asked the accomplice to come and be your assistant. You seem to have made up your mind that the girl isn't in it."

"Bless her little innocent heart, no."

"You sound pretty ghastly sentimental about her." Malcolm looked at him disgustedly. "What's she like?"

"Well, she's skinny. Her elbow went into me like a spike every time she nudged me at the movies."

"I don't think," remarked Clara, who was quietly engaged on her *bouillon*, "that *I'd* better do that to him. I don't think he'd care for it from me."

"You're not skinny enough," said Malcolm.

"She has nice bright eyes," continued Gamadge, "not

very large. Her hair—well, she does the best she can with it, but you can't do much at home, nowadays. She catches cold easily, poor little thing. The tip of her nose is always red; she tried to make powder stick on it last night, but . . ."

Malcolm was now laughing to such an extent that he couldn't swallow.

"And she loves to ride in taxis," said Gamadge, "and I wish her taste in sandwiches was better. Still, they're cheap."

Clara said calmly: "Henry loves her because she's a victim and doesn't resent it."

"Doesn't know it," Gamadge corrected her. "There's nothing more beautiful than a martyr who isn't aware of the fact." He picked up Clara's hand and held it against his cheek. As he laid it down again, she said: "I can't imagine what you mean."

"*That's* what I mean." Gamadge was laughing too.

"So now the accomplice is Welsh," said Malcolm, restored to the use of his voice, "and he's a mental case, and you're giving him the run of the laboratory. What kind of situation does that remind you of, Clara?"

"Frankenstein. Is he a mental case, Henry?"

"Not being a psychiatrist, I don't know what he is. There are other people in the world besides Welsh who might have been involved at the Bradlock studio, and might have watched me come, and gone and changed that brandy flask."

"It's Welsh," insisted Malcolm. "He'll blow you all up. That's the accident I was talking about. No, seriously, Gamadge, you might spare your family these risks. This fellow is devoted to Mrs. Paul Bradlock. You don't suppose that story you told him about the annuity on the hundred thousand dollars is going to prejudice him all in a minute? He's asked her about it, and she's explained everything. And as you say, they've read the papers."

Old Theodore came to the door of the library. He said: "Mist' Gamadge, young man downstairs say he came about a job. Mist' Gamadge, we *has* a veteran."

They had a veteran, a war-worn mechanic's mate, who

in spite of his battered condition seemed to run the whole house, inside and out, with little assistance from Theodore. Gamadge said: "Ask him to wait a few minutes in the office. Or has he had his lunch?"

"I'll ask him."

"See if he minds having it in the kitchen with Youmans. If he does, bring a tray for him up here. Just explain that he'll get it quicker and hotter that way. Tell him it's not a precedent."

"I can explain in a satisfactory manner, Mist' Gamadge."

"I know you can."

Theodore left the room. Three faces, void of expression, turned back to their contemplation of food. There was a heavy silence.

Theodore returned. "He only wanted coffee, he and Youmans they's talking boats together."

"When he's had his coffee, bring him up here."

The Gamadges and Malcolm were finishing their own coffee when Theodore ushered Welsh into the library. He stood, looking huge in his clean slacks, glancing not at the people in the room, but about him; at the polychrome ceiling, the old Turkey rug, the globes, the books, the portrait over the mantel. Then he turned his eyes on the group in the window. Gamadge and Malcolm rose.

"Glad you came, Mr. Welsh. Clara, Mr. Welsh; this is Mrs. Gamadge, and Mr. Malcolm."

Welsh nodded twice.

"Came to look the job over, did you?"

"That feller off the P.T. boat, he showed me the laboratory."

"We might go down."

Welsh said: "Vera—Mrs. Bradlock thought it would be a good idea for me to come."

"I'm glad she approves. But you can't manage three jobs, you know. That's impossible."

"I'm leaving. Going room-hunting this evening." He glanced about him again. "Sally Orme is coming in later—like you said."

"That's nice," said Clara. "Won't you have a cigarette?"

"I have mine, Ma'am."

"You go on down," said Gamadge. "Be with you as soon as I've finished this. Know the elevator?"

"Pretty cute." Welsh slowly smiled. He nodded again, turned, and went out. When they heard the elevator, Clara said: "That boy is lost."

"Getting his bearings."

With no further words, Gamadge went down.


# 16

# Appointments


Welsh stood in the door of the laboratory, cats weaving in and out around his feet. He said: "I've decided to take the job."

"That's fine. Be a big help to me. Just now there isn't much doing, but a little later on"—Gamadge went over to his office desk—"we'll be swamped. Big collection from an estate, and the deceased seems to have bought everything in sight. We fear he didn't take advice. Let's see now, about terms."

Welsh came forward, and they settled that. "Want to start as of now?" asked Gamadge.

"If I can."

"Good." They went into the laboratory, where Welsh had been unshrouding apparatus. He said: "Nice place."

"Hope you'll feel at home here. Later on, when you give up the hospital job and go back to Columbia, you can work here in the evenings if you like. They'll certainly make some arrangement for you, you know."

Welsh said, adjusting the screws of a microscope: "Suppose I'm never able to make a living."

"You're doing that now." Gamadge was looking through papers in a drawer. "Do you type?"

"Yes."

"That'll be a help, too. You understand how to enlarge photographs?"

"I can do it."

"These things have to be photographed and enlarged."

Welsh was interested. "What are they?" He picked up a mounted letter carefully.

"This is a letter by a seventeenth-century divine, who has suddenly become fashionable enough to be faked. This is the possible fake. We have to compare them in every way."

"How do you know which is the real McCoy?" asked Welsh, looking closely at them both.

"This one has been in recipient's family ever since it was written, when nobody would have bothered to fake it."

"Ever since . . ."

"They wanted money and sold their stuff. If you're going to work in here you ought to have an overall. There isn't a blouse in the place that would go on you; Theodore can let you have something to keep your clean slacks from getting smeared up."

Welsh laid the letters down, and turned to the big camera. He said: "Youmans is a nice guy, isn't he?"

"Yes. I wanted you to meet him. That's why I—but you probably realized it."

"I don't care where I eat."

"If you want to ask me anything, I'll be in the office out there. Here's the telephone, and there's the dark-room. It used to be a pantry, and this was the dining-room. We're not particular either."

Welsh laughed. Gamadge said: "You know you're a lucky devil." The other raised his dark eyes, and Gamadge went on: "To have a friend like Sally Orme."

"Some people wouldn't see it."

"Some people are fools. What a disposition. What a smile."

"She thinks a lot of you, too."

"I'm glad she made up her mind so soon."

Welsh leaned against a corner of a table. He said: "You're way off about Vera—Mrs. Bradlock."

"That so?"

"She told me about that money. She explained the whole business. She didn't want a lot of questions asked about that manuscript or whatever it was. I don't blame her. She says Bradlock came by it honestly, she made inquiries and nothing's been stolen. She needed the cash. She's making plans to go away, West, and get into a business with a friend."

"Is she?"

"She figures Bradlock owed her the chance to take a rest and look around, and so do I." He turned away, and then came back. "I meant to ask you—you were in the papers this morning. Any reason you'd rather I didn't talk about it?"

"Talk away, why not."

"It's just that you didn't mention it before, that's all."

"Never occurred to me to mention it."

"Did they grill you?"

"Grill me? Why should they?"

"Well, you were there just before and after."

"It's supposed to be a suicide."

"Was it really something you talked about?"

Gamadge said: "I didn't think Mrs. Wakes seemed particularly depressed when I left. I was astounded when I found her dead."

"Vera—I showed her the paper. She'd already seen the item. She says her husband may have known Mrs. Wakes in Paris, but she didn't." Welsh looked up at Gamadge. "Would you do that?"

"Kill myself?" Gamadge was lighting a cigarette. When it was burning, he took it out of his mouth and answered: "None of us knows that answer. I'd have to be in a bad way, though, not to wait for tomorrow. I'm convinced of that much."

After a long pause Welsh said: "So would I."

The chow, Sun, walked in, sauntered up to Welsh and delicately touched his nose to the young man's out-stretched hand.

"I see you know the approach," said Gamadge.

"Sure, let them see what they're up against before you start pawing them. You have a nice dog there."

"He's my wife's. The cats are mine."

"Get along together?"

"Very well indeed."

Welsh turned to the camera. Gamadge went back to the office, closing the door after him. He found Malcolm, coat on and hat in hand, in the hall doorway.

Gamadge said: "He's hired."

"Seems all right to me. But—"

"He wasn't here under orders to get the job at all costs. Couldn't you see that?"

"Well, I did think so."

"He's too big to be an accomplice. Might as well send a water buffalo around tampering with evidence. Can't you find him a room? You know real-estate people."

"I'll ring them."

"Two rooms," said Gamadge. "One for Miss Orme."

Malcolm, laughing, went away. Gamadge sat down at his desk and rang Indus.

Indus answered: "Did it go all right?"

"Couldn't have been more of a success. Now I want to talk to the lady of the house. I think the two young people will be otherwise engaged until dinner time. Would you go up there and see if the coast is clear, and meet me at the gates, say at six o'clock?"

"Don't you want my report first?"

"Have you one?"

"I was interested. Funny layout, I wanted to see it in the daytime. I went up there around nine o'clock this morning. She started out from the annex at nine thirty, morning paper under her arm."

"Did she look as if she'd had a shock?"

"What can you tell from a face like that? Had on a dowdy rig, old tweed suit and pull-on felt. She made a beeline down town by bus for that walk-up in the Fifties—where the Iverson guy lives."

"She'd want to talk to him."

"She was there best part of an hour, and he came out on the street with her afterwards. He looked mighty bad."

"That's good news."

"And her face was all screwed up. I don't think they

had much fun out of the visit. By the time they parted he was mad clear through. He went back in the walk-up, and she hailed a cab. I got one just behind, and we went down by the East Side Drive to William Street, and she went into the City and Seaboard Trust Company."

"No!"

"Did I do right to take the cab down? You didn't give me no assignment for to-day."

"That's because I was afraid you'd tire yourself out for nothing."

"This kind of thing don't tire me. I kept the cab, because they don't come easy down there. She was in the bank some time, came out with her big handbag under her arm and hanging on to it with both hands too, the way the women do when they've got something valuable in tow."

"Perhaps that hundred thousand isn't salted away in an annuity after all."

"What?"

"Never mind. Go ahead, I'm all ears."

"I couldn't find out of course if she cashed a cheque, or got something out of deposit, or what. I'd have lost my cab."

"We'll have to use our imaginations."

"She rode right home, and then she came out again and went down town to Fifth Avenue and had a shopping tour. Bought the stores out, she was loaded down with boxes."

"She's getting ready for a trip."

"I saw her home, and she looked so dog-tired that I thought she'd probably stay there. Anyway, I called it a day and had lunch."

"Indus, I don't know what to say."

"I enjoyed it."

"Will you meet me up there at six o'clock?"

"Tell you what, I'll be down in that service alley beside the apartment house. Nobody can see me there from the annex, that great high wall with the spiked railing runs all the way through to the next street. If anybody comes out of the annex I can *be* walking through to the next street."

"Good idea. I'd like to catch her alone. Watch out for Iverson."

Gamadge put down the telephone. It rang immediately, and he picked it up again. Avery Bradlock's voice came to him clearly:

"Mr. Gamadge? This is Avery Bradlock."

"Yes, Mr. Bradlock."

"This morning I saw that paragraph in the paper about a Mrs. Wakes; and your being there just before and after—"

"Yes. I was there."

"I think my brother knew these people, in Paris. Most extraordinary thing, what on earth could have induced her to—did you foresee it at all? Was she—"

"I was dumbfounded when I found her dead. Couldn't believe it."

"Must have been upsetting for you."

"Well, it was, rather."

"Vera—my sister-in-law—said she had never met Mrs. Wakes or her husband. At first I wondered whether you had gone there on account of something that was said at dinner the other night."

"To be quite frank, I did get to thinking about your brother's Paris friends, and all that circle."

"I'd like very much to talk to you about it. There's a lot of business at the office just now; I play bridge regularly at the club every day until about seven, but if I might call in before that . . . Or would you find it too inconvenient to drop in at the house for a cocktail?"

"As a matter of fact, I'll be in that neighbourhood."

"That's most kind of you. If you get there before I do, my wife will entertain you for me. Thank you very much."

Gamadge replaced the telephone and went upstairs; he told Clara that within the next two hours, for reasons strategical as well as humane, he must have a housing list for Thomas Welsh and if possible for Miss Orme.

From that moment there was feverish activity upstairs and down. While Thomas Welsh—oblivious of the hell popping on his behalf all around him—worked quietly behind his closed doors and in the dark-room, Gamadge and Clara looked up numbers and called them. They called welfare centres, housing bureaux, Clara's relatives and all their available friends. Youmans was sent out to consult with neighbourhood tradesmen and with the partolman on the beat. Theodore, and Athalie the cook, came to the library with reminders of distant rooming houses and model tenements which had sheltered Gamadge's assistants in the past.

By half-past four Gamadge had several addresses. Clara's aunt Vauregard had supplied that of a former housekeeper in Queens, who wanted a respectable young man for her spare bedroom who would be quiet at night. (Welsh filled requirements there, as few other young men could.) Somebody else knew of some young people in Jackson Heights who had clubbed together to buy a house, and hadn't filled the top story. Elena Malcolm came through with a lively suggestion from a Brooklyn matron whose son was willing to enter into a kind of Box and Cox arrangement with Welsh—Welsh to occupy the young man's bedroom from morn till eve, while the son was working like everybody else at the normal hours. There was a couple in the Bronx with two rooms and a bath just vacated by a couple who had moved up in the income brackets and down in the residential areas; they wanted another couple, but frankly preferred them married.

Throughout the campaign, Malcolm's real-estate friends naturally preserved a dignified silence.

At twenty minutes to five Gamadge pronounced himself satisfied. At a quarter to five Theodore came up and said a young lady was calling. "And tea is on the way."

"Good. Bring her up," said Gamadge, "and tell Mr. Welsh to knock off for refreshments."

Miss Sally Orme entered the library shyly, was greeted by Clara, and introduced to the animals. Welsh appeared, followed by Theodore and the tea tray.

"And all we need," observed Gamadge, as they sat around Clara's gate-leg table, "is that nice young man that works in the bank."

The young man who worked in the bank provided facetious small talk until the party had settled down comfortably to a solid meal of tea and toast, thin sandwiches and cakes. Theodore said that there were some buns coming. Athelie just had them out of the oven.

The housing list was exhibited. Clara thought that the place in the Bronx was the best proposition of the lot, wasn't it possible? Welsh said it was all right as far as he was concerned. Gamadge imagined that the landlords might be satisfied with an engagement, if they had it in writing. Youmans appeared in the doorway, chewing, with a belated offer from a seaman friend to share his folks' living-room, put another cot in, but the consensus of opinion in the library was that Welsh's hours might not entirely fit the seaman's folks' household arrangements.

Young Henry, brought in by his nurse, leaned against his father's knee and ate toast. The animals lay about, leaving it up to the human race not to step on them.

Sally Orme said they'd better not stay too long, with all these places to look at. "And if I did find a place, too, it would be all right; because Vera's going away."

"Is she really?" Gamadge avoided his wife's eye. He passed cake. "Mr. Welsh said something, but I didn't know it was settled."

"Tom doesn't know either. She just got a telegram from her friend in Los Angeles. The friend has a florist's store, and Vera can buy into it with that thousand dollars she got for those letters."

Welsh sat quietly busy with his second cup of tea; he bent down and picked up a piece of toast which young Henry had dropped on the floor.

"She'll be a partner," said Sally. "She's all excited, and she's packing now. I wish Tom was there to help her get her things out of the attic, but we ought to find somewhere to live."

"Yes," said Welsh. "Seems so."

"Anyway, she hasn't much to pack, everything there belongs to the Avery Bradlocks."

Welsh sat back on the chesterfield. "Guess she just can't help keeping her business to herself," he said. "I had a taste of what she went through, that night her husband nearly broke the Avery Bradlocks' bow window. Remember, Sally?"

"Yes, I do."

"Hated them—Paul Bradlock did. Well, Avery kept him pretty short of cash." He turned to Sally and put a hand on hers and smiled. "It's all over now."

"And the agency is going to get me a position in an office."

Clara detached young Henry from the group and took him away. At the door she said: "I'm rather sorry Dave Malcolm went home. He would have been so interested."

Sally rose. "We ought to go, Tom."

"But I haven't finished my trick downstairs."

"Don't worry about that," said Gamadge. "First day and all. The important thing is for you both to get somewhere to live."

They took the list and went away. Gamadge accompanied them to the door; when he closed it after them the telephone in the office was ringing. It was Indus jubilant:

"She's in there alone, Mr. Gamadge. The kid left, and she went out herself to post letters, and now she's back in there. I couldn't swear to it, but I'd say she was in there alone."

"Be up in a few minutes, Indus."

"I'll be down in that service alley. Then if anybody did go in the annex, I could duck out and warn you."

"Thanks. I'll see you."

Gamadge hurried to the second floor. He told Clara that he was going out to a cocktail party at the Bradlocks'. "And you're *still* not asked."

"Henry," she said, as he hastily prepared himself for his outing, "those little things are all right."

"Even Tiny Tom?"

"I like him. I'm so glad they're getting away. If you never do anything more in this case, you did that."

"Well, it does look a little that way." He laughed, kissed her, and ran downstairs. At the corner of the street he took a cab.

# 17

# Informal

Gamadge dismissed the cab at the Bradlocks' corner. He walked past the apartment house slowly, getting out a cigarette. At the top of the service steps he paused to light it.

Indus remained below. He said: "Nobody went in, nobody came out." Turning, he squinted up at the side wall of the studio; almost flush with the wall and railing, it showed two narrow and tall windows and a higher, smaller one beyond. Indus said: "It's a kind of an ugly little place, squatting there."

"Vampires might live in it."

"That's so."

"Come up a minute."

Indus, on the top step, took a light from Gamadge, while the latter talked low. Indus nodded, nodded again, grinned, threw away his cigarette unsmoked, and after a few more words from Gamadge came up to the street level. Gamadge, after a glance around him, went back a little way towards the corner. Indus walked through the iron gates and along the flagged path to the studio door. An insignificant little figure, frail and ageing, he yet looked businesslike and full of assurance. He had some papers in his hand, and he took a pencil out of his pocket and inserted it behind his ear.

He rang at the studio door. After a wait, Mrs. Paul Bradlock opened it. She looked impatient and preoccupied. Her hair was done up in a cotton bandanna, and she wore a pink overall apron, creased and dusty.

Her hand on the knob, she asked shortly: "What is it?"

"Mr. Welsh in?"

"No."

"I'm calling about that metallographic and petrographic microscope."

"The what?"

"Mr. Welsh ordered it on approval." Indus fumbled among papers.

"I don't know anything about it."

"He gave us a deposit. Am I to collect, or leave it, or take it away? It's a special," said Indus, his face crumpled with earnestness. "Pre-war stock."

"He didn't say a thing." Mrs. Bradlock was annoyed. "He might have left a cheque or something."

"He's always rushing off somewhere. I've been out all morning myself. I haven't seen him."

"It's a special," insisted Indus. "He wouldn't get another for I don't know how long."

"I certainly can't take the responsibility of paying for it."

"Well, Ma'am, he might not want to lose it. He might have left a cheque."

"Cheque? No. I can't run his business for him," said Mrs. Bradlock angrily. "Well, I'll look in his room. He didn't say anything about it, and I didn't see a package."

"Delivered to the hospital."

"Oh. Well, wait a minute."

Mrs. Bradlock left Indus in the doorway, and went across the room to the little stair. The trap at the top of the upper flight was open, luggage was strewn about the living-room. The place looked bare and dismantled; papers blew about the floor from the draught that Indus was letting in through the open door.

As she mounted the stair Indus made a gesture behind him without turning.

Mrs. Bradlock reached the gallery and disappeared into a room on the right. After a minute she came back and leaned over the gallery rail.

"I can't—"

She stopped, her hands gripping the wood. The front door was closed, and instead of the little figure of the salesman a taller man stood looking quietly up at her.

Her face empty of colour, she asked harshly: "What does this mean?"

Gamadge said: "It's all right, Mrs. Bradlock, no cause for alarm. I thought you might possibly see me coming, and decide to be out." He walked half-way across the room towards the stairs, and stopped.

"I certainly would have been 'out.' I'm busy. What is this?" Her hands on the rail were trembling.

"I won't detain you, I'm not here to prevent you from going where you like, or taking your money with you."

"What do you want?" she almost screamed at him.

"Well, you might guess. You probably read your paper this morning. I came for that document you got out of your safe deposit box at the City and Seaboard Trust."

"You damned spy, are you a thief too?"

"No, just interested in old documents. This one can't fairly be said to belong to you—your husband blackmailed it out of Mrs. Wakes the night he died. Iverson killed him for it, and one of you poisoned her before she could talk to me about it. But I had already seen her, you know. Do you think *I* imagined it was suicide?"

She steadied herself, closing her eyes. When she opened them she spoke more firmly: "You're quite mad. I have no such thing."

"You haven't disposed of it; you wouldn't destroy it. Just let me have it, Mrs. Bradlock, and I'll give you my word that I'll make no more inquiries in this case. Unless I talk to them, the police won't go on with it."

She laughed, suddenly and loudly.

"Perhaps it is funny," said Gamadge. "But I'm not compounding a felony. The police have all the suggestions that I could give them, and if they don't follow up, that's not my fault. I won't go on prodding them. I don't feel called upon to avenge these deaths, you know. All I want is that document—or documents."

"I suppose you think you know what it is!"

"I'll guess, if you like."

Her eyes went past him. He looked around, to see Iverson standing a little behind him. Iverson had a hand in the pocket of his lounge coat, and he had the stance of one about to act violently. He straightened, smiled, and said calmly: "Our expert."

Mrs. Bradlock shrieked at him: "I told you not to show him that thing! It's all your stupid fault!"

Iverson's face was clay-coloured. He said: "Well, that can be remedied."

"Oh, for heaven's sake," protested Gamadge, "not *another* fatality! Oh, no; that would be one too many. The police department couldn't swallow three. And there's that little man I sent to get me into the place; he knows I came. He'd make a horrible row."

"Still," said Iverson, "I feel really tempted."

"Were you tempted last night?"

"Er—if I'd known what I knew later I'd have been seriously tempted."

"But weren't you?" Gamadge smiled at him.

"Well, to be frank, yes; but there was a dog."

Vera Bradlock came down the steps. She was fumbling at her breast, under the apron. She said: "I can't stand this. Hill, you are so stupid. Don't you see he won't go on with it? But if we don't give it to him he'll never let us go."

Iverson said sharply: "Wait a minute, wait a minute."

"No!" She ran down the last few stairs, snatched something out from under the bib of the apron, and pushed it into Gamadge's hand. It was a yellow envelope, not very long or large, and much worn and soiled.

Gamadge looked inside, reading between half-opened pages. Then he flattened the envelope again and put it in his pocket. "No," he said, looking from her to Iverson, "you have my word. But I'll give you a tip in exchange—don't hurry out of town. It won't look well. And if the police question me, I won't hold out on them."

"Oh, for God's sake get out of here," said Iverson in disgust. "You know as well as I do that there's no evidence even now. It's just that I don't want Vera breaking down on me."

"It's all your fault," she was screaming again as Gamadge left the annex. He shut the door on her parrot voice.

Out on the street Indus lurked, expectant. Gamadge

said: "Like a charm. All right, Indus, call it a day, and you
get a big bonus for this morning. But Mr. Iverson put one
over."

"You mean he was there all day?"

"It's not your fault, you know; I didn't warn you that he
knew the Avery Bradlocks well enough to call, and that he
might get a chance to fake an exit and slip through by the
connecting way."

Indus looked heartbroken. "I knew a cab drove up, but
it stopped at the Bradlock house, and I never popped out to
look. I won't take no bonus. Just give me the bare time."

"Don't be silly. Send me the bill and I'll do what I like
about it."

"You goin' home? We might ride—"

"No, I have an engagement at the Avery Bradlocks'."

They parted, Indus still crestfallen. Gamadge left him
looking sadly through the iron gates. He himself went on,
and up the Bradlock steps.

# 18

# Cocktail Party

The parlourmaid recognized Gamadge with a smile.
He said: "I know I'm very early; Mr. Bradlock—"

"He's not home yet, sir, but Mrs. Bradlock is up in her
sitting-room. That's where they have their cocktails when
there's no party."

"I'm glad I'm no party."

"No dinner party, I meant, sir." She took his hat and
coat, and then preceded him up the broad stairs, which
were uncarpeted for the summer and shining. A solemn,
conventional house, with little character except its respectable solidity. Perhaps it reflected the original owner's own
character, as well as his taste.

But Mrs. Bradlock had done something to her sitting-room. Far from modernistic, it had a brightness and a knowingness. Brilliant colours mitigated the north light, there were French flower engravings on the walls and a remarkable landscape over the mantel. Mrs. Bradlock herself, advancing to meet Gamadge, was wearing a long, informal dinner dress of dark green, with a braided belt in many colours.

She said: "I'm so glad you could come. What would you like to drink?"

Gamadge shook hands with her. He said: "Well, to tell you the truth I'd like an old-fashioned; but don't hurry it for me."

"I'll have one with you." She glanced at the parlour-maid, who hurried off.

"Mother rests until seven," said Mrs. Bradlock. "You'll have to put up with me. Let's sit down."

There was a settee in front of the fire, and two armchairs flanking it. She sat in a corner of the little sofa, and Gamadge took the chair on her right. He looked up at the picture above the chimney piece. "Isn't that a beauty?"

"Yes. I used to want to paint like that." She smiled.

"Did you work at it?"

"In a ladylike way."

They laughed, and discussed modern painting. The parlourmaid brought the tray, set a little table in front of Mrs. Bradlock, and departed. Gamadge said: "I'm rather glad we have a chance for a little talk together. I've brought you something."

She looked surprised. Her glass in her hand, she met his eyes wonderingly. "Something for me?"

"Yes. Take a good swallow of that first."

"Why?" She frowned a little, not much liking this.

"To please me."

His expression was so friendly that she smiled too, and drank some of her old-fashioned. Then she put the glass down, still looking doubtfully at him. He said, his hand inside his coat, "Your own property. Yours for keeps now," and brought out the yellow envelope. She took it from him, looked inside it, pulled out two papers and stared at them.

One fell to the floor. Ignoring it, she crushed the other up in her hand, and gave him a wild look.

"It's all right," he said gently.

Suddenly, like a sand picture dissolving under the pull of the tide, her very personality crumbled and disintegrated before his eyes. She leaned forward, elbows on knees and face against her clenched hands, shaking with sobs.

After a moment he got up and came forward. "Take some more of this," he said, offering her the glass. "I ordered it for you, you know."

She looked up at him, tears running down her face. Then she got out her handkerchief and wiped them away, took the glass from him in her left hand, keeping the paper crushed in her right, and drank some of the whisky. She said in a strangled voice: "I don't understand how you—"

"Never mind that just now. Shall we get rid of it first?" He motioned with his head towards her clenched fist. She opened her hand and held it out, as if it held a horror.

"Good. I see you know friend from foe." Gamadge took the paper, lighted a corner of it, and held it up the chimney. When it was all but consumed, he laid the charred fragment on top of the wood in the fireplace, broke it up with the shovel, and pushed the remains behind the logs.

"And that's all of that." He picked up the other paper from the floor, a dwarf-sized letter sheet, and looked at it. "As for this, it could break your heart."

She had pulled herself together. "I don't know how often it's nearly been the end of me."

"It's perfectly harmless now. Might I just keep it for a few days? Work of art."

She shuddered. He put it in his wallet, sat down again and drank some whisky.

"But how did you—how *could* you—" she was sitting back now; a little colour had risen in her face, she looked years younger.

"I stopped in at the studio and made a little bargain with your friends. I'd seen Mrs. Wakes before she died—"

"I know. I can't understand."

"You will. Those two in the studio didn't know what

she might have told me; so I said that if they'd let me have
the incriminating documents I'd call it square and leave the
rest to destiny. They didn't like the idea of inquiries,
naturally; I suppose you realize that I know they killed
her?"

She said faintly: "I can't see *how* you knew."

"Well, they made a bad mistake. They showed me
something—it was probably one of Brandon's projects—
which put me on to the fact that they were part of a forgery
ring. I connected that fact with another—Wakes's facilities
for research and so on in England. Never mind the details.
I'll just say that Mrs. Wakes told me nothing."

"She wouldn't. Poor thing, she never would have given
Paul that thing if he hadn't threatened her. He heard about
it from Wakes, and he knew she had it. He knew all about
the forgeries from Vera."

"I supposed so."

"Then two years ago Avery got so sick of him, and all
the frightful things that happened more and more often;
and he told Paul they'd have to go, and that Paul must get
himself cured or there wouldn't be any more money. Paul
told me he was going to get that letter of mine, and the
thing you have, from Mrs. Wakes, and use it to make me
persuade Avery to keep them there in the studio. *He* didn't
ask me for money."

"But after he was killed they did?"

"They've had everything Avery ever gave me. Avery
said that if he died there might be delays, there always
were in settling an estate, and he used to give me bonds
that I could sell when I needed them. He'll never know
they're gone." Tears welled up in her eyes again. "My
mother won't know. Is it really all over?"

"Those people will never bother you again."

"Vera told me to-day that she was going, but that I'd
have to send her—I had nothing left but my allowance and
my jewellery."

"You know, I can't understand why Mrs. Wakes ever
kept the thing," said Gamadge. "Here, let's smoke; it'll be a
pacifier."

He lighted a cigarette for her, and went on: "The

Wakes woman seemed a good sort. I can't understand her keeping that letter, since she wasn't using it for blackmail."

"But she kept it for protection. She was so afraid that some day she might be accused of the forgeries, it might all come out; and she thought that if she had one of my forgeries, and that letter of mine to Jeremy about it, it would prove I did them, and Avery would do anything to protect me and them all."

Gamadge reflected. He said: "Fear can do pretty awful things to people. So can remorse. Don't think she didn't suffer from it!"

"But I don't see how you thought of *me*, Mr. Gamadge." She looked at him, half frightened. "They protected me so—I mustn't be suspected, or they'd lose their power over me. They made me pretend to be against them, to be making Avery keep Vera there in the studio because I thought we owed it to her."

"Yes, you fronted for them very well. But"—Gamadge looked at the end of his cigarette—"somebody had to change those brandy flasks."

She put a hand up over her face. "Oh God, they made me do it."

"I don't know how you did."

"I had to go, and she was dead."

"How did you get in?"

"Hilliard Iverson had got a duplicate key."

"Somebody had to go," repeated Gamadge, "and I thought someone had gone after I got there yesterday afternoon; to clamp their alibi. They wouldn't trust a paid employee, and I got the impression that the little Orme girl and Welsh weren't responsible. But you could have seen me from that side window—if you were watching."

"I was watching."

"That's what we call corroborative detail, you know. The important questions for me were provided by the blackmailers themselves. They had a lot of money; if, as I thought, they got it by blackmail, whom were they blackmailing? And why, if she had a lot of money, did Mrs. Paul Bradlock stay on in the studio and show no signs of wanting to leave it?"

"They stayed to watch me."

"To keep their grip on you. Well, you'd been in Paris during the crucial years, you might have met your husband through Paul Bradlock."

"I did. He introduced us."

"And you'd had financial reverses—or your family had had them. I thought it added up," said Gamadge. "I found that it did when I glanced at the contents of that envelope."

She looked at it, lying on the table. "Why did you do it for me, Mr. Gamadge, if you're not going to do anything more? Why?" She asked it almost timidly. "You know what I've done—you guessed it before."

"I don't like blackmailers; and don't you think you've worked out a sentence, Mrs. Bradlock?"

"I've been dying for two years. I've been in agony."

"You looked"—Gamadge smiled at her—"so frozen."

"If I hadn't loved Avery it wouldn't have been so frightful."

"And Paul Bradlock knew you loved him. No, I have no wish to avenge Paul Bradlock's murder."

She shrank back. "Was it one? I often thought—"

"We couldn't prove it. You know, he needed killing; he could blackmail you, because he wouldn't have cared if you had been shown up—he wouldn't have cared on your account or on his brother's."

"I was so afraid of him. Mr. Gamadge—"

"Yes, Mrs. Bradlock."

"Shall I tell you how it happened?"

"I'd like to know."

"I was so happy in Paris—Mother left me there with friends, and I had everything, and I was so happy. Then I got word that the money was gone, and that I had to come home. I had to leave everything and come home to lost, ruined, poverty-stricken Longridge. And Jeremy Wakes—he went everywhere—I'd met him, and he'd seen the Christmas cards and things I did for fun, imitating old scripts, you know. And he asked me if I wanted to make enough money to keep me in Paris, just a little work in my spare time."

She laughed. "He said it wasn't like forging cheques, it

was just giving people something they wanted, no harm
done, everybody happy. I knew what I was doing; I made
up my mind that if people would pay such prices for things
when other people had nothing, they deserved what they
got. I did a lot of the forgeries. Jeremy and Mr. Brandon
and Mrs. Wakes and a lot of them worked together, and I
knew some of the people who did the actual work, like me.
It was quite exciting."

Her voice was sardonic. "Quite exciting. Then I met
Avery, and I came home and was married, and somebody
wrote me that Mr. Brandon had killed himself, and why.
After Jeremy died, Mrs. Wakes wrote—she said she
thought everything would be all right, but she was keeping
my letter.

"Then, two years ago, Paul told me he was going to put
pressure on. When he was killed I thought it was all over,
but Vera . . ." Her voice died. "She got so much fun out of
it."

"Yes. Neurotic personality. I'm afraid we'll have to let
her get away with those bonds of yours, Mrs. Bradlock."

"If you knew how thankful I am to let her have them!
They made me ask you to come on Monday evening, Mr.
Gamadge. They said Avery mustn't suspect that I was
against it. I didn't understand what they'd been doing."

"Iverson is just a fellow-worker in the vineyard?"

"That's all. He used to bring things back here from
Paris and sell them."

"They're not pleased with each other just now."

A door closed below. She got up. "That's Avery."

"You're all right, Mrs. Bradlock?"

"All right."

Avery Bradlock came into the room. "Gamadge, I hope
they've been treating you properly?" He glanced at the
little table. "I see you've had something. For me, a cocktail.
I've told Ellen, my dear."

She went up to him and kissed him.

"Well!" He turned to Gamadge, laughing, his arm
around her. "What a welcome! Hanged if I know why. She
ought to be in the sulks at me, I'm so late; but then she
never is out of temper. Pretty good record?"

"Pretty good." Gamadge, in high good humour, stood with his hands in his pockets, contemplated them benignantly and congratulated himself. "Tell you the truth, Mr. Bradlock, I'm not so popular at home just now as you are. I forgot that we had a dinner engagement, and I've got to change for it. That's why I came so early."

"Oh, don't run off yet. I've asked Ellen to go over and see whether my sister-in-law can't join us. She's heard from a friend in California, and she's packing for the trip; but she'd like to meet you again, I know, and hear about this unfortunate woman."

"I can't tell you much about Mrs. Wakes, Mr. Bradlock. Really not more than you saw in the papers. I went there to get up some material for a paper on the twenties in Paris—or did I tell you?"

Mrs. Bradlock said: "Don't keep him, darling. He might come another time, and Mrs. Gamadge might come too. For dinner, you know."

"Good idea. Well—"

Steps pounded on the stairs. Ellen came to the door, leaned against the jamb, and stood gasping. Her eyes were starting from her head, her mouth open.

Bradlock stared too. "What on earth—"

"It's killed she is. It's killed she is."

"What do you mean?" He went over and put a hand on her shoulder. "What are you talking about, Ellen?"

"She fell down her little stairs." Ellen burst out into loud weeping. "She must have been getting her luggage out, and she fell."

Mrs. Bradlock stood rigid. Bradlock said over his shoulder: "Stay here, Nannie. Keep your mother out of it," and ran for the stairs. Gamadge followed him; down to the first floor, through into the back entry, along the connecting way. Both doors were wide.

The studio was dark before them. Then, as they paused just inside, find their eyes adjusted themselves to the twilight, they saw the insignificant sprawl at the foot of the stairway across the room. It seemed no more than a flattened heap of dusty clothes, at first; in a moment more it had taken on the look of a discarded and broken manikin.

# 19

# Accident

Bradlock strode over open suitcases and went down on one knee beside the dead woman. Gamadge followed slowly; his eyes took in the open trap-door two stories above, the little dressing case near the body, the outflung hands. Bradlock twisted his head and looked up: "She's dead."

"Yes."

"It looks as if she'd broken her neck. My God, poor little creature. Is there any—I'd better turn her. Can't see her face."

Gamadge said nothing. Bradlock hesitated, looked up at the open trap, around at Gamadge again. "Frightful accident. She must have fallen the whole two flights, to get smashed like this. Carrying that thing?" he glanced at the dressing case. "This place has a ban on it." He put his hand on the crumpled pink sleeve of the overall, drew it back. "I don't know what to do first."

"Call your doctor," suggested Gamadge. "He'll take over, he'll know the procedure."

Bradlock, relief showing on his face, got up. "Good idea. I only hope he's at home."

While he got the number, Gamadge stood leaning against the piano; gravely sympathetic, but decently withdrawn and to all appearances at ease. Bradlock, waiting for an answer to his call, turned and looked at him. "Look here, you have a dinner engagement. Oughtn't to keep you."

"I'll stand by till somebody comes."

"Would you shut and lock that door?"

Gamadge did so.

"I suppose there's nobody else here?" Bradlock glanced up at the gallery doors. "But there can't be, unless

135

that fellow—who is it? Walsh? Welsh?—unless he's asleep up there."

"I'll look. Don't think so."

Gamadge came forward, circled the body, and went up to the gallery. He looked into two dark cubicles, each with a view of old bricks and mortar some two feet away. He came back. "Nobody."

"Fleming is on his way, thank fortune. Gamadge, this is a tragedy. That unfortunate little soul—Fleming says not to touch her . . ."

"No, these accidents ought to be filed away properly from the start."

"Glad that occurred to me—subconsciously, perhaps. This poor little soul; she was using that thousand dollars Iverson paid her for the letters to buy into a florist's business in Los Angeles. Would you think they'd need florists? More than anybody, it seems. She called me up about it only this afternoon. Couldn't wait for help, I suppose, all excitement over the move, and look what happens. Peculiar, independent little thing." He sat beside the telephone, casting disgusted looks about him. "This place is disgraceful, but she never said so. I'm inclined to think my mother-in-law is right, they like to live in a mess." He paused. "Once or twice I tried to get in, while she was out; look things over. But the door was always bolted on this side—I got an idea she didn't want us here."

"Some privacy fixation, perhaps?"

"She may have had some feeling of resentment. It was a difficult situation while my brother was alive—I suppose you know. Everybody did. Insoluble problem. With the best will in the world, what could I do? Like dealing with a—with a madman. You can't help them. Money lost or stolen, or spent on—perhaps I was hard on him. Nannie thought so. Tell you the truth, I was glad she was going."

"Much better."

"Well, she's gone with a vengeance!" He glanced with pity and a certain revulsion at the body. "Can't pretend we ever liked her. We're not intellectuals. I hope Fleming can save us more newspaper headlines. Do you think—"

The doorbell rang. Gamadge admitted a stoutish man, carrying a black bag. He exuded competence and authority.

"Well, well, well, Bradlock, this is too bad."

"Yes, pretty ghastly. Mr. Gamadge, Doctor Fleming. Gamadge was having a cocktail with us when we got the news."

Fleming went directly across to the body. After a minute he got up, and took Bradlock's place at the telephone. "Been dead a very short time," he said, dialling. "Killed instantly, I should say. May have broken every bone in her body, besides her neck." He talked into the telephone, replaced it, and turned. "Fell from up there, did she? Looks as if she had that little case in her hand; they can be heavy if they're filled. Sorry it had to happen to you, Avery. Bad luck."

Bradlock said: "Mr. Gamadge has a dinner engagement."

Fleming nodded at Gamadge. "You go on home, then. No need to keep you here. With the Bradlocks when the maid brought the news? Go on home."

"Well, if I can't help—"

"Not a thing to do but wait for the green light. You have it now, beat it. There's a pile of routine."

Gamadge shook hands with Bradlock, and went back through the connecting way. He got his hat and coat, hurried out of the Bradlocks' front door, and passed the radio car at the corner.

When he reached home he dashed upstairs to the library. "Get your things, Clara, we're dining out."

"Out? Where? Those Bradlocks?"

"No, that's for some other night; you're invited at last." He was out in the hall, telephoning. Malcolm answered. "That you, Dave? We're on our way? You invited us to dinner."

"We certainly did not," replied Malcolm with indignation. "The Lithuanian has gone for her night out, and we're hacking pieces off a cold ham and opening cans. And there isn't enough cold ham for us, much less you."

"We'll bring the dinner."

Gamadge slammed down the receiver and made for

the kitchen. A few minutes later Athalie the cook, in-
furiated, was wrapping a hot roast chicken in waxed paper.

"And we always meant to dine out," Gamadge told her,
"only we forgot. And all Theodore has to say is that we are
out, and he doesn't know where."

"If he know where," said Athalie, pushing the chicken
into a carton, "he got the second sight. Want gravy in a milk
container? You friends must be trash."

Ten minutes more saw the Gamadges tumbling into a
cab.

After dinner the four played bridge. Gamadge seemed
fascinated by the game. "We're not the kind of people to eat
and run," he explained. "Come on, another rubber."

Nobody could get any kind of explanation out of him.
They left at eleven, Gamadge having won all the money.
"My luck's running," he said. "I need it."

When he and Clara got home a visitor was waiting for
them, and Gamadge showed no surprise. It was Lieutenant
Durfee, and he had made himself comfortable on the
chesterfield. He rose slowly as they entered.

"Hello," said Gamadge, "how are you? I'm glad
Theodore made you feel at home."

"Least he could do." Durfee shook hands with Clara.
"Me waiting here an hour."

"Well, I'm glad it's a social call. It would be, of course,"
said Gamadge, "since you're—er—taking refreshment."

"You think you're funny."

Clara said she was a little tired, and bade them good
night. When she had gone Durfee sank back on the
chesterfield.

"Now, let's have it," he said. "Why did you duck out
before we got there?"

# 20

# Money's Worth

Gamadge, pouring himself a drink, raised his head to register surprise. "There? You mean up at the Bradlocks'?"

"That's it."

"I ducked out before *you* got there? What's Homicide doing at an accident?"

"Nothing. I'm talking for the department."

Gamadge, highball in hand, studied him with eyebrows arched high. "Didn't they tell you I was over at the other house? Didn't they explain that I had a dinner engagement?"

"Yes." Durfee crossed one foot over the other, clasped his hands behind his head, and gazed at the ceiling. "All in all, the Bradlocks are news. When I caught the accident I couldn't help wondering whether you being there didn't make some kind of a tie-up."

"*You* thought there was a tie-up? Suffering cats, what next?" Gamadge drank deep.

"I know, I know. I've reformed," said Durfee.

"But why reform now, when it was an ac—"

Durfee flapped a hand at him. He asked: "Suppose somebody was up at the top of a little flight of stairs like that, just climbed out of a trap-door, with a suitcase in one hand. What would you do if you didn't like the party, and you were standing down below in the living-room, and you thought it would be nice if they fell down the two flights and broke their neck?"

Gamadge thought it over. "I'd throw something at them."

Durfee burst out laughing. "Anything funny?" asked Gamadge, rather shocked.

"You are. That must have been what happened.

139

Nobody could be up there behind her, no string across the stairs—she'd been going up and down right along, getting out her suitcases. You're a nice-dressed caller down below, you don't want to get mussed up or anything. So you pick up a little fitted case, heavy as all get-out, and you take a swing. Hit her full in the face. Face is all bruised up, the whole front of it; Doc says she couldn't very well do that falling. You try it."

Gamadge sat on the edge of the table and swung his foot. "I don't believe any M.E. would come to any such conclusion without reasons for it better than that one."

"You're right. Don't worry about the Bradlocks. Nice folks, ain't they? Bradlock's chauffeur drove him right home from his club and rang the doorbell for him and saw him in, and that was at a little after seven."

"I know he got home then, because I looked—"

"Sure, sure. He was playing bridge at his club, he was put into his car there by his chauffeur and the doorman. What a lot of help Mr. Bradlock does need, don't he?

"Then Mrs. B., she was talking to you from the time her maid left her after she dressed for dinner. The other maid was in and out picking up after the first maid. What a lot of help—"

"Oh, forget it."

"As for you, of course you might have fitted it in on your way up from here, nobody keeps track of *your* hours, but we got another line that looks even better."

"I'm relieved."

"Don't you want to know what it is?"

"Well, yes; I'm interested."

"Now, mind you, I haven't changed my opinion about the Wakes suicide. That was suicide. You got her scared, and my opinion is that when the rest of the gang saw your name in the papers they worried. You started a general break-up. What the racket is we probably never will know."

"Won't we?" Gamadge looked disappointed.

"Not if you don't."

"I told you—"

"Yes, and thank God I don't have to work on it."

"Why not?"

"I love to hear you asking the questions for a change," said Durfee. "There's a little retired op named Indus. Nice little feller, used to be with Geegan. He takes a walk up town in the park of an afternoon, and to-day he was walking past the Bradlock place on his way to the Madison Avenue bus. He sees a man come out of the Bradlock studio, plenty quiet and careful, sees him walk along that side yard to the gates as if he was walking on eggshells, sees him squint up at the Bradlocks' bow window there and duck by—can't help ducking. Being an op, Indus is interested. He walks along, and sees the feller dive down into that service alley beside the apartment house. Being an op, he looks at the time. It's six twenty-five."

Gamadge's foot had stopped swinging.

"Well, what does Indus do but chase after him, and I can tell you there wasn't a better man at it in New York in his day. There's something about the feller that interests him. They go along to the next street down, then east, then a few blocks down, and they're on that block beside that old abandoned hospital with the high wall and the big trees. Know it?"

"I ought to. It's Saint Damian's."

"It is. I remember, you know it. Well, the feller has a bad conscience, so he does notice Indus on that stretch. He lets him catch up, there under that wall, dark and deserted stretch, and what do you know? He pulls a gun on him."

"No!"

"For a fact, this Iverson pulls a gun. But this Indus—slick little customer, knows all the tricks—he dives, tackles him, and has him flat with the gun sliding across the pavement. He hollers murder, and people begin running. Iverson gets away from him, of course, and has his gun again. What does he do? Puts a bullet in his own head."

Gamadge was now able to form sentences. "What in the world," he wondered aloud, "should he do that for?"

"Well, for one thing," said Durfee, "he had his pockets stuffed with government bonds with Mrs. Bradlock's name penciled on the top of the covers, the way those banks or brokers do. He was bulging with them. Didn't have more than time to grab them and get out. Then in the second place, he left the studio at just about the wrong time for him and the right time for us. Left with her property in his pockets and inside his vest. And he'd fixed himself by pulling the gun. Personally, I think this Indus ought to get some kind of a reward."

"You think so because you won't have to check up on the details now?" Gamadge laughed.

"Are *you* going to check up any more?" Durfee looked amused too.

"No, of course not. They're all dead—I can't do any checking."

"That's so. Given up looking for that accomplice, have you? The one that changed the brandy flask?"

"There was none, of course."

"You actually admit it?"

"Can't I be wrong sometimes?" asked Gamadge.

"This time you could. It wasn't that little girl that beat it when you got to the studio this afternoon?"

"No. Ridiculous."

"Or that boy?"

"Certainly not."

"I thought you'd backed down on it when Bradlock told me about your going up there on invitation this evening to tell him about poor Mrs. Wakes. Not a word out of you to them about all this brandy-flask stuff, or anything else. So," said Durfee, "I didn't give you away."

"You didn't? Fine. Now they may ask me to dinner."

"They were all pretty well laid out by the Iverson business. Upset Mrs. Bradlock a good deal."

"Naturally it would."

"But that old lady they got up there—the mother-in-law; bright as a button, isn't she? She was all excitement. Told me about how they never got into the studio, and all the rest of it."

"Yes, she's always full of useful information."

"They were sitting around after dinner when I got there. I had to drop in, of course, about Iverson and the twenty-odd thousand he took off Mrs. Paul Bradlock."

Gamadge turned a little away, picked up his glass, and drank some whisky. He said after a pause: "He'd have had his share before, if it was loot. Er—Bradlock wouldn't know anything about any such amount as that. Are you turning it over to him?"

"Bradlock? He won't handle it, won't even listen about it. Says it's no business of his, belongs to her heirs. Old Lady Longridge pipes up that it probably goes to this little cousin, Miss Orme."

Gamadge suddenly grinned. "I bet it is Sally's!"

"Bradlock wasn't interested in how she got it or where it came from or whether Iverson killed her for it. I guess he'd be only too glad to let sleeping dogs lie. And we didn't find any evidence about it in the studio, or in Iverson's place either—not even a burned paper."

Gamadge was recovering his spirits a little. "No, you wouldn't."

"I guess you were right about that, anyhow," conceded Durfee. "They'd dug up something of value in Paul Bradlock's papers. It was obvious that Avery Bradlock didn't know a thing about any of it."

"He doesn't."

"Well," Durfee rose. "As you say, they're all dead— Paul Bradlock, Mrs. Paul, Mrs. Wakes and Iverson. Listen, Gamadge, do me one favour."

"Any number."

"Don't get interested in my affairs. Three people dead in two days, two suicides and one probably murder. Keep away from me, will you? You're poison."

"In homœopathic doses, perhaps . . ."

"Not any way."

They laughed, shook hands, and went out into the hall. Gamadge let him go down in the elevator alone. As the front door closed behind him the telephone tinkled, and Gamadge snatched it up.

"Mr. Gamadge?" Indus sounded subdued.

"Indus, for heaven's sake, I'd have burst into a thousand shreds if you hadn't called."

"I couldn't get away any sooner, not to make it safe."

"Thank goodness you didn't call half a minute ago."

"I thought you might be tied up, too. I'm round the corner. Could I—"

"I think it's all right now. Be careful."

"You bet."

Gamadge was down at the front door when he came. He drew him into the hall, into the office, took his hat and coat away from him, and sat him in a chair. Indus, his hands on his knees, looked up with an odd expression on his squirrel face; half pride, half doubt. Gamadge sat down in front of him.

"Indus, I don't understand any of it. Why should you go after Iverson? Why should he shoot himself? What happened to your joints?"

"I didn't tell it just the way it happened, Mr. Gamadge. And the cops don't know about my jernts."

"So I gathered."

"I couldn't have caught up with the feller down there by the hospital wall, not if he'd pulled a gun and beat it away. I pulled my gun first."

Gamadge sat back. "Well, that's explained. But—"

"He'd seen me in the studio, before you got there. Must have come through that passage you told me about."

"He did."

"Anything said about his being at the Bradlocks'?"

"Thank God no, the maid wasn't around when Durfee called."

"Well, when we got down on that block I was across the street and behind him, and he turned and saw me. He could have got away easy, of course, so I had to pull my gun and tell him to stop. Then when I got up to him he pulled his, but I tackled him first and down he went."

"But—"

"I told him I saw him do it."

"Do what?"

"Throw that case at that woman and knock her down the stairs."

"You—how could you see it?"

"Well, after you left I thought I might as well be on hand, report proceedings if there were any. It just occurred to me that if I climbed along that railing that runs along the top of the wall, I could see in one of those side windows of the studio."

Gamadge said nothing.

"I know I didn't have orders," said Indus mildly. "But I hadn't thought of the window while you were there. I climbed along, and I saw her come out of the trap-door and stand up there with a case in her hand, yelling at him. I didn't hear what she said. He was looking up at her, and if I'd been in her place I wouldn't have taken the risk."

"I have an idea she was getting ready to throw him over. *She* hadn't committed the murders."

"Anyway, she said too much. He just stooped down and picked up that little case and swung it. I couldn't look."

Gamadge sat motionless.

"Down she came, I took one peek at her, and I saw him go over and start hunting in the ruins. I beat it out of there and waited for him along the block. Was he fixing to lam out with the money? Or was he satisfied with the accident picture?"

"I don't know. The accident picture would give him a good start. I don't think he'd stay around afterwards. No, you're right, he was clearing out. He had the whole works—his and hers."

"I don't know about that. All I know is, I wasn't sure if you'd want me to tell it this way."

Gamadge rose. "Indus, if nobody saw you—"

"I'll bank on that."

Gamadge began feverishly to hunt in his desk, unlock a filing cabinet, gather up currency. "Here; here's the bonus. Send me the bill."

"Mr. Gamadge." Indus sat with his hands full of money, looking at it. "It ain't worth this much."

"That's what you think."

"I wasn't follering orders."

"Do you think I wouldn't have given orders, if I'd imagined that you could get a look through that window? Indus, we're not concealing anything useful—everybody knows it's murder, and there's nobody left alive to be prosecuted. If they really started asking me questions, one thing leads to another, and—Indus, Avery Bradlock doesn't know anything about this business. I'm going to keep him from knowing, if it's the last thing I do."

Indus thought it over for a minute, and then let it sink away and be lost in the depths of his discretion. He asked: "Who's going to pay you back?"

"Nobody. It's worth the money."

Indus nodded, and got up. Gamadge saw him out, then he came back, woke Sun the chow, put his leash on, and walked him around the block. It was a clear, pleasant night, and the air was fresh and clean in Gamadge's nostrils; Iverson was dead, Vera Bradlock was dead, and they hadn't pulled the other house down with them to destruction— Mrs. Avery Bradlock, Avery Bradlock, or the mother-in-law who was so fond of him.

When he came upstairs, Clara spoke from the dark: "Everything all right?"

"I think so. I'm a little tired."

# 21

# Autograph Letter Signed

On a misty October evening, warm as summer, J. Hall came to dinner with the Gamadges. Afterwards, while they drank their coffee and Hall told Clara stories, Gamadge considered some of the matters that had been settled, or were in a fair way to being settled, since he had last seen his learned friend.

The Bradlock studio was fast turning into a bijou residence. Windows had been punched into its north and south walls, the Bradlock house had been sealed off, and the connecting passage (also provided with windows) was now a kitchenette. The old kitchen was a bedroom. Decorators were doing the place up in brilliant colours, and prospective tenants were already outbidding one another in fierce rivalry for possession.

Bradlock having stonily refused to do anything whatever about the securities found on Iverson's body, his position being that if his sister-in-law had sold property of his brother's it had been hers to sell and now belonged to her heirs, Welsh had appealed to Gamadge in Sally's behalf. Gamadge had recommended a young lawyer. Since nobody else laid claim to the bonds, the young lawyer had finally argued them into a safety deposit box under the name of Sara Orme Welsh. Iverson's share had not been found; he had probably converted it into cash, and banked it somewhere under another name; Gamadge could only hope that if it was found it would not add up to anything likely to attract the attention of Avery Bradlock. But would anything, even mathematics, persuade Avery Bradlock into suspicion of his wife? Gamadge thought not.

The irony involved in this struggle to get the bonds out of the Bradlock family was known to only two persons, and neither of them was likely to comment on it to anybody else. Not even to each other. When the Gamadges did dine with the Bradlocks the conversation was general, and old Mrs. Longridge kept a firm hand on the helm. She was not likely to steer the talk into dark waters, and when she did refer to the studio it was remotely, as "our other house." She rather sounded as if their other house might be very far off, as far as Longridge itself.

Welsh spent his afternoons in the Gamadge laboratory, his mornings at other technical work. He had given up the hospital, and slept of nights. Sally typed in an office. When they left the Bronx, they had settled in the suburbs. Sally wished to spend her fortune on his education, but he thought not. He could soon enough pay for that himself.

All in all, Gamadge thought, prospects were cheerful so far as he and his friends were personally concerned. Now J. Hall was speaking to him:

"Gamadge, what about that investigation of yours—that Chaucer thing? Anything come of it?"

"Nothing at all."

"I wondered at the time—you mentioned Paul Bradlock. His wife was killed, not twenty-four hours after our talk."

"Oh, the interval was longer than that."

"I always meant to call you up about it, but I'm so busy."

"Don't know a thing."

J. Hall laughed.

"Tell you what, though." Gamadge rose. "I have something to show you. An acquisition." He opened the desk drawer and found an envelope among other papers. It was a plain white envelope, and it contained a dwarf-sized letter sheet covered with writing. An undistinguished hand—or perhaps the script of an invalid?

J. Hall took it and looked at it. "Beautiful," he said. "Beautiful specimen. His last lap, poor fellow. Which is it?" He studied it, and looked up. "Do you know, Gamadge, I can't recall ever having seen this one, original or facsimile. Good heavens, is it a new find? Where did you—do you want me to sell it for you?"

"Well, no." Gamadge held out his hand for it. "There was a letter with it, but that's lost. I never read it."

"But this doesn't need any statement of provenance." Hall reluctantly handed it back.

"I thought you'd say it didn't."

Gamadge opened the letter, held it by a corner, and clicked his cigarette lighter. Hall started forward in his chair; his arm shot out convulsively.

"Good heavens, Gamadge, what are you doing?"

The flame lighted salutation and signature: *My dearest Fanny*, and at the end, *John Keats*.

"Burning it up," said Gamadge. "It's a forgery."

## ABOUT THE AUTHOR

ELIZABETH DALY was born in 1878 in New York City. The daughter of a judge and niece of the famous playwright and producer Augustin Daly, she grew up immersed in the world of literature and the theatre. Miss Daly received her B.A. from Bryn Mawr College in 1901 and her M.A. from Columbia the following year. She later returned to Bryn Mawr as a reader in English and remained there for two years, adding to her duties the coaching and producing of amateur plays. Although she began her literary career at the age of sixteen and published light verse and prose in various magazines, she did not write her first mystery novel until she was past sixty. In 1940, *Unexpected Night* was published and marked the first appearance of Henry Gamadge, her famous bibliophile detective. Miss Daly considered the detective novel at its best a high form of literature and didn't seek to write any other kind of fiction. Elizabeth Daly was a very popular writer in the United States as well as England, where Gamadge was dubbed "the American Peter Wimsey." One of her greatest fans was the grande dame of English mystery herself, Agatha Christie.

# Masters of Mystery

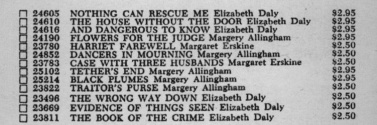

# WHODUNIT?

**Bantam did! By bringing you these masterful tales of murder, suspense and mystery!**